Murder on the Orient Express

Agatha Christie is known throughout the world as the Queen of Crime. Her books have sold over a billion copies in English with another billion in 100 foreign languages. She is the most widely published author of all time and in any language, outsold only by the Bible and Shakespeare. She is the author of 80 crime novels and short story collections, 19 plays, and six novels written under the name of Mary Westmacott.

Agatha Christie's first novel, *The Mysterious Affair at Styles*, was written towards the end of the First World War, in which she served as a VAD. In it she created Hercule Poirot, the little Belgian detective who was destined to become the most popular detective in crime fiction since Sherlock Holmes. It was eventually published by The Bodley Head in 1920.

In 1926, after averaging a book a year, Agatha Christie wrote her masterpiece. *The Murder of Roger Ackroyd* was the first of her books to be published by Collins and marked the beginning of an author-publisher relationship which lasted for 50 years and well over 70 books. *The Murder of Roger Ackroyd* was also the first of Agatha Christie's books to be dramatised – under the name *Alibi* – and to have a successful run in London's West End. *The Mousetrap*, her most famous play of all, opened in 1952 and is the longest-running play in history.

Agatha Christie was made a Dame in 1971. She died in 1976, since when a number of books have been published posthumously: the bestselling novel *Sleeping Murder* appeared later that year, followed by her autobiography and the short story collections *Miss Marple's Final Cases*, *Problem at Pollensa Bay* and *While the Light Lasts*. In 1998 *Black Coffee* was the first of her plays to be novelised by another author, Charles Osborne.

Agatha Christie

Murder on the Orient Express

HARPER

HARPER

An imprint of HarperCollins *Publishers*
1 London Bridge Street, London,
SE1 9GF, United Kingdom
www.harpercollins.co.uk

This *Agatha Christie Signature Edition* published 2007
16

First published in Great Britain by
Collins 1934

ISBN-13: 978-0-00-728263-0

Fiction / Mystery

Typeset by Palimpsest Book Production Limited,
Grangemouth, Stirlingshire

Printed and bound in India by
Thomson Press India Ltd.

To M.E.L.M. Arpachiya, 1933

Contents

Part 3

Hercule Poirot Sits Back and Thinks

Part 1

The Facts

Chapter 1

An Important Passenger
on the Taurus Express

It was five o'clock on a winter's morning in Syria. Alongside the platform at Aleppo stood the train grandly designated in railway guides as the Taurus Express. It consisted of a kitchen and dining-car, a sleeping-car and two local coaches.

By the step leading up into the sleeping-car stood a young French lieutenant, resplendent in uniform, conversing with a small lean man, muffled up to the ears, of whom nothing was visible but a pink-tipped nose and the two points of an upward curled moustache.

It was freezingly cold, and this job of seeing off a distinguished stranger was not one to be envied, but Lieutenant Dubosc performed his part manfully. Graceful phrases fell from his lips in polished French. Not that he knew what it was all about. There had been rumours, of course, as there always were in such cases. The General – *his* General's – temper had grown worse and worse. And then there had come this Belgian stranger – all the way from England, it seemed. There had been a week – a week of curious tensity. And then certain things had happened. A very distinguished officer had committed suicide, another had resigned – anxious faces had suddenly lost their anxiety, certain military precautions were relaxed. And the General – Lieutenant Dubosc's own particular General – had suddenly looked ten years younger.

Dubosc had overheard part of a conversation between him and the stranger. 'You have saved us, *mon cher*,' said the General emotionally, his great white moustache trembling as he spoke. 'You have saved the honour of the French Army – you have averted much bloodshed! How can I thank you for acceding to my request? To have come so far –'

To which the stranger (by name M. Hercule Poirot) had made a fitting reply including the phrase, 'But indeed do I not remember that once you saved my life?' And then the General had made another fitting reply to that disclaiming any merit for that past service, and with more mention of France, of Belgium, of glory, of honour and of such kindred things they had embraced each other heartily and the conversation had ended.

As to what it had all been about, Lieutenant Dubosc

was still in the dark, but to him had been delegated the duty of seeing off M. Poirot by the Taurus Express, and he was carrying it out with all the zeal and ardour befitting a young officer with a promising career ahead of him.

'Today is Sunday,' said Lieutenant Dubosc. 'Tomorrow, Monday evening, you will be in Stamboul.'

It was not the first time he had made this observation. Conversations on the platform, before the departure of a train, are apt to be somewhat repetitive in character.

'That is so,' agreed M. Poirot.

'And you intend to remain there a few days, I think?'

'*Mais oui*. Stamboul, it is a city I have never visited. It would be a pity to pass through – *comme ça*.' He snapped his fingers descriptively. 'Nothing presses – I shall remain there as a tourist for a few days.'

'La Sainte Sophie, it is very fine,' said Lieutenant Dubosc, who had never seen it.

A cold wind came whistling down the platform. Both men shivered. Lieutenant Dubosc managed to cast a surreptitious glance at his watch. Five minutes to five – only five minutes more!

Fancying that the other man had noticed his surreptitious glance, he hastened once more into speech.

'There are few people travelling this time of year,'

he said, glancing up at the windows of the sleeping-car above them.

'That is so,' agreed M. Poirot.

'Let us hope you will not be snowed up in the Taurus!'

'That happens?'

'It has occurred, yes. Not this year, as yet.'

'Let us hope, then,' said M. Poirot. 'The weather reports from Europe, they are bad.'

'Very bad. In the Balkans there is much snow.'

'In Germany too, I have heard.'

'*Eh bien*,' said Lieutenant Dubosc hastily as another pause seemed to be about to occur. 'Tomorrow evening at seven-forty you will be in Constantinople.'

'Yes,' said M. Poirot, and went on desperately, 'La Sainte Sophie, I have heard it is very fine.'

'Magnificent, I believe.'

Above their heads the blind of one of the sleeping car compartments was pushed aside and a young woman looked out.

Mary Debenham had had little sleep since she left Baghdad on the preceding Thursday. Neither in the train to Kirkuk, nor in the Rest House at Mosul, nor last night on the train had she slept properly. Now, weary of lying wakeful in the hot stuffiness of her overheated compartment, she got up and peered out.

14

This must be Aleppo. Nothing to see, of course. Just a long, poor-lighted platform with loud furious altercations in Arabic going on somewhere. Two men below her window were talking French. One was a French officer, the other was a little man with enormous moustaches. She smiled faintly. She had never seen anyone quite so heavily muffled up. It must be very cold outside. That was why they heated the train so terribly. She tried to force the window down lower, but it would not go.

The Wagon Lit conductor had come up to the two men. The train was about to depart, he said. Monsieur had better mount. The little man removed his hat. What an egg-shaped head he had. In spite of her preoccupations Mary Debenham smiled. A ridiculous-looking little man. The sort of little man one could never take seriously.

Lieutenant Dubosc was saying his parting speech. He had thought it out beforehand and had kept it till the last minute. It was a very beautiful, polished speech.

Not to be outdone, M. Poirot replied in kind.

'*En voiture, Monsieur,*' said the Wagon Lit conductor.

With an air of infinite reluctance M. Poirot climbed aboard the train. The conductor climbed after him. M. Poirot waved his hand. Lieutenant Dubosc came

15

to the salute. The train, with a terrific jerk, moved
slowly forward.

'*Enfin!*' murmured M. Hercule Poirot.

'Brrrrr,' said Lieutenant Dubosc, realizing to the
full how cold he was . . .

II

'*Voila, Monsieur.*' The conductor displayed to Poirot
with a dramatic gesture the beauty of his sleeping
compartment and the neat arrangement of his luggage.
'The little valise of Monsieur, I have placed it *here.*'

His outstretched hand was suggestive. Hercule Poirot
placed in it a folded note.

'*Merci, Monsieur.*' The conductor became brisk and
businesslike. 'I have the tickets of Monsieur. I will also
take the passport, please. Monsieur breaks his journey
in Stamboul, I understand?'

M. Poirot assented.

'There are not many people travelling, I imagine?'
he said.

'No, Monsieur. I have only two other passengers – both English. A Colonel from India, and a
young English lady from Baghdad. Monsieur requires
anything?'

Monsieur demanded a small bottle of Perrier.

Five o'clock in the morning is an awkward time to board a train. There was still two hours before dawn. Conscious of an inadequate night's sleep, and of a delicate mission successfully accomplished, M. Poirot curled up in a corner and fell asleep.

When he awoke it was half-past nine, and he sallied forth to the restaurant-car in search of hot coffee.

There was only one occupant at the moment, obviously the young English lady referred to by the conductor. She was tall, slim and dark – perhaps twenty-eight years of age. There was a kind of cool efficiency in the way she was eating her breakfast and in the way she called to the attendant to bring her more coffee, which bespoke a knowledge of the world and of travelling. She wore a dark-coloured travelling dress of some thin material eminently suitable for the heated atmosphere of the train.

M. Hercule Poirot, having nothing better to do, amused himself by studying her without appearing to do so.

She was, he judged, the kind of young woman who could take care of herself with perfect ease wherever she went. She had poise and efficiency. He rather liked the severe regularity of her features and the delicate pallor of her skin. He liked the burnished black head with its neat waves of hair, and her eyes, cool, impersonal and grey. But she was, he decided, just a little too efficient to be what he called '*jolie femme.*'

Presently another person entered the restaurant-car. This was a tall man of between forty and fifty, lean of figure, brown of skin, with hair slightly grizzled round the temples.

'The colonel from India,' said Poirot to himself.

The newcomer gave a little bow to the girl.

'Morning, Miss Debenham.'

'Good-morning, Colonel Arbuthnot.'

The Colonel was standing with a hand on the chair opposite her.

'Any objection?' he asked.

'Of course not. Sit down.'

'Well, you know, breakfast isn't always a chatty meal.'

'I should hope not. But I don't bite.'

The Colonel sat down.

'Boy,' he called in peremptory fashion.

He gave an order for eggs and coffee.

His eyes rested for a moment on Hercule Poirot, but they passed on indifferently. Poirot, reading the English mind correctly, knew that he had said to himself, 'Only some damned foreigner.'

True to their nationality, the two English people

were not chatty. They exchanged a few brief remarks, and presently the girl rose and went back to her compartment.

At lunch time the other two again shared a table and again they both completely ignored the third passenger. Their conversation was more animated than at breakfast. Colonel Arbuthnot talked of the Punjab, and occasionally asked the girl a few questions about Baghdad where it became clear that she had been in a post as governess. In the course of conversation they discovered some mutual friends which had the immediate effect of making them more friendly and less stiff. They discussed old Tommy Somebody and Jerry Someone Else. The Colonel inquired whether she was going straight through to England or whether she was stopping in Stamboul.

'No, I'm going straight on.'

'Isn't that rather a pity?'

'I came out this way two years ago and spent three days in Stamboul then.'

'Oh, I see. Well, I may say I'm very glad you are going right through, because I am.'

He made a kind of clumsy little bow, flushing a little as he did so.

'He is susceptible, our Colonel,' thought Hercule Poirot to himself with some amusement. 'The train, it is as dangerous as a sea voyage!'

Agatha Christie

Miss Debenham said evenly that that would be very nice. Her manner was slightly repressive.

The Colonel, Hercule Poirot noticed, accompanied her back to her compartment. Later they passed through the magnificent scenery of the Taurus. As they looked down towards the Cilician Gates, standing in the corridor side by side, a sigh came suddenly from the girl. Poirot was standing near them and heard her murmur:

'It's so beautiful! I wish – I wish –'

'Yes?'

'I wish, I could enjoy it!'

Arbuthnot did not answer. The square line of his jaw seemed a little sterner and grimmer.

'I wish to Heaven you were out of all this,' he said.

'Hush, please. Hush.'

'Oh! it's all right.' He shot a slightly annoyed glance in Poirot's direction. Then he went on: 'But I don't like the idea of your being a governess – at the beck and call of tyrannical mothers and their tiresome brats.'

She laughed with just a hint of uncontrol in the sound.

'Oh! you mustn't think that. The downtrodden governess is quite an exploded myth. I can assure you that it's the parents who are afraid of being bullied by *me*.'

They said no more. Arbuthnot was, perhaps, ashamed of his outburst.

'Rather an odd little comedy that I watch here,' said Poirot to himself thoughtfully.

He was to remember that thought of his later.

They arrived at Konya that night about half-past eleven. The two English travellers got out to stretch their legs, pacing up and down the snowy platform.

M. Poirot was content to watch the teeming activity of the station through a window pane. After about ten minutes, however, he decided that a breath of air would not perhaps be a bad thing, after all. He made careful preparations, wrapping himself in several coats and mufflers and encasing his neat boots in goloshes. Thus attired he descended gingerly to the platform and began to pace its length. He walked out beyond the engine.

It was the voices which gave him the clue to the two indistinct figures standing in the shadow of a traffic van. Arbuthnot was speaking.

'Mary –'

The girl interrupted him.

'Not now. Not now. When it's all over. When it's behind us – *then* –'

Discreetly M. Poirot turned away. He wondered.

He would hardly have recognized the cool, efficient voice of Miss Debenham . . .

'Curious,' he said to himself.

The next day he wondered whether, perhaps, they had quarrelled. They spoke little to each other. The girl, he thought, looked anxious. There were dark circles under her eyes.

It was about half-past two in the afternoon when the train came to a halt. Heads were poked out of windows. A little knot of men were clustered by the side of the line looking and pointing at something under the dining-car.

Poirot leaned out and spoke to the Wagon Lit conductor who was hurrying past. The man answered and Poirot drew back his head and, turning, almost collided with Mary Debenham who was standing just behind him.

'What is the matter?' she asked rather breathlessly in French. 'Why are we stopping?'

'It is nothing, Mademoiselle. It is something that has caught fire under the dining-car. Nothing serious. It is put out. They are now repairing the damage. There is no danger, I assure you.'

She made a little abrupt gesture, as though she were waving the idea of danger aside as something completely unimportant.

'Yes, yes, I understand that. But the *time*!'

'The time?'

'Yes, this will delay us.'

'It is possible – yes,' agreed Poirot.

'But we can't afford delay! The train is due in at 6.55 and one has to cross the Bosphorus and catch the Simplon Orient Express the other side at nine o'clock. If there is an hour or two of delay we shall miss the connection.'

'It is possible, yes,' he admitted.

He looked at her curiously. The hand that held the window bar was not quite steady, her lips too were trembling.

'Does it matter to you very much, Mademoiselle?' he asked.

'Yes. Yes, it does. I – I must catch that train.'

She turned away from him and went down the corridor to join Colonel Arbuthnot.

Her anxiety, however, was needless. Ten minutes later the train started again. It arrived at Haydapassar only five minutes late, having made up time on the journey.

The Bosphorus was rough and M. Poirot did not enjoy the crossing. He was separated from his travelling companions on the boat, and did not see them again.

On arrival at the Galata Bridge he drove straight to the Tokatlian Hotel.

Chapter 2

The Tokatlian Hotel

At the Tokatlian, Hercule Poirot asked for a room with bath. Then he stepped over to the concierge's desk and inquired for letters.

There were three waiting for him and a telegram. His eyebrows rose a little at the sight of the telegram. It was unexpected.

He opened it in his usual neat, unhurried fashion. The printed words stood out clearly.

'*Development you predicted in Kassner Case has come unexpectedly please return immediately.*'

'*Voilà ce qui est embêtant,*' murmured Poirot vexedly. He glanced up at the clock.

'I shall have to go on tonight,' he said to the concierge. 'At what time does the Simplon Orient leave?'

'At nine o'clock, Monsieur.'

'Can you get me a sleeper?'

'Assuredly, Monsieur. There is no difficulty this time of year. The trains are almost empty. First-class or second?'

'First.'

'*Trés bien, Monsieur.* How far are you going?'

'To London.'

'*Bien, Monsieur.* I will get you a ticket to London and reserve your sleeping-car accommodation in the Stamboul-Calais coach.'

Poirot glanced at the clock again. It was ten minutes to eight.

'I have time to dine?'

'But assuredly, Monsieur.'

The little Belgian nodded. He went over and cancelled his room order and crossed the hall to the restaurant.

As he was giving his order to the waiter a hand was placed on his shoulder.

'Ah! *mon vieux*, but this is an unexpected pleasure,' said a voice behind him.

The speaker was a short, stout elderly man, his hair cut *en brosse*. He was smiling delightedly.

Poirot sprang up.

'M. Bouc.'

'M. Poirot.'

M. Bouc was a Belgian, a director of the Compagnie Internationale des Wagons Lits, and his acquaintance with the former star of the Belgian Police Force dated back many years.

'You find yourself far from home, *mon cher*,' said M. Bouc.

'A little affair in Syria.'

'Ah! And you return home – when?'

'Tonight.'

'Splendid! I, too. That is to say, I go as far as Lausanne, where I have affairs. You travel on the Simplon-Orient, I presume?'

'Yes. I have just asked them to get me a sleeper. It was my intention to remain here some days, but I have received a telegram recalling me to England on important business.'

'Ah!' sighed M. Bouc. '*Les affaires – les affaires!* But you – you are at the top of the tree nowadays, *mon vieux*!'

'Some little success I have had, perhaps.' Hercule Poirot tried to look modest but failed signally.

Bouc laughed.

'We will meet later,' he said.

Hercule Poirot addressed himself to the task of keeping his moustaches out of the soup.

That difficult task accomplished, he glanced round him whilst waiting for the next course. There were only about half a dozen people in the restaurant, and of those half-dozen there were only two that interested Hercule Poirot.

Agatha Christie

These two sat at a table not far away. The younger was a likeable-looking man of thirty, clearly an American. It was, however, not he but his companion who had attracted the little detective's attention.

He was a man of between sixty and seventy. From a little distance he had the bland aspect of a philanthropist. His slightly bald head, his domed forehead, the smiling mouth that displayed a very white set of false teeth, all seemed to speak of a benevolent personality. Only the eyes belied this assumption. They were small, deep set and crafty. Not only that. As the man, making some remark to his young companion, glanced across the room, his gaze stopped on Poirot for a moment, and just for that second there was a strange malevolence, and unnatural tensity in the glance.

Then he rose.

'Pay the bill, Hector,' he said.

His voice was slightly husky in tone. It had a queer, soft, dangerous quality.

When Poirot rejoined his friend in the lounge, the other two men were just leaving the hotel. Their luggage was being brought down. The younger was supervising the process. Presently he opened the glass door and said:

'Quite ready now, Mr Ratchett.'

The elder man grunted an assent and passed out.

'*Eh bien*,' said Poirot. 'What do you think of those two?'

'They are Americans,' said M. Bouc.

'Assuredly they are Americans. I meant what did you think of their personalities?'

'The young man seemed quite agreeable.'

'And the other?'

'To tell you the truth, my friend, I did not care for him. He produced on me an unpleasant impression. And you?'

Hercule Poirot was a moment before replying.

'When he passed me in the restaurant,' he said at last, 'I had a curious impression. It was as though a wild animal – an animal savage, but savage! you understand – had passed me by.'

'And yet he looked altogether of the most respectable.'

'*Précisément*! The body – the cage – is everything of the most respectable – but through the bars, the wild animal looks out.'

'You are fanciful, *mon vieux*,' said M. Bouc.

'It may be so. But I could not rid myself of the impression that evil had passed me by very close.'

'That respectable American gentleman?'

'That respectable American gentleman.'

'Well,' said M. Bouc cheerfully. 'It may be so. There is much evil in the world.'

Agatha Christie

At that moment the door opened and the concierge came towards them. He looked concerned and apologetic.

'It is extraordinary, Monsieur,' he said to Poirot. 'There is not one first-class sleeping berth to be had on the train.'

'*Comment?*' cried M. Bouc. 'At this time of year? Ah, without doubt there is some party of journalists – of politicians –?'

'I don't know, sir,' said the concierge, turning to him respectfully. 'But that's how it is.'

'Well, well,' M. Bouc turned to Poirot. 'Have no fear, my friend. We will arrange something. There is always one compartment – the No. 16, which is not engaged. The conductor sees to that!' He smiled, then glanced up at the clock. 'Come,' he said, 'it is time we started.'

At the station M. Bouc was greeted with respectful empressement by the brown-uniformed Wagon Lit conductor.

'Good-evening, Monsieur. Your compartment is the No. 1.'

He called to the porters and they wheeled their load half-way along the carriage on which the tin plates proclaimed its destination:

ISTANBUL TRIESTE CALAIS

'You are full up tonight, I hear?'

'It is incredible, Monsieur. All the world elects to travel tonight!'

'All the same, you must find room for this gentleman here. He is a friend of mine. He can have the No. 16.'

'It is taken, Monsieur.'

'What? The No. 16?'

A glance of understanding passed between them, and the conductor smiled. He was a tall, sallow man of middle age.

'But yes, Monsieur. As I told you, we are full – full – everywhere.'

'But what passes itself?' demanded M. Bouc angrily. 'There is a conference somewhere? It is a party?'

'No, Monsieur. It is only chance. It just happens that many people have elected to travel tonight.'

M. Bouc made a clicking sound of annoyance.

'At Belgrade,' he said, 'there will be the slip coach from Athens. There will also be the Bucharest-Paris coach – but we do not reach Belgrade until tomorrow evening. The problem is for tonight. There is no second-class berth free?'

'There *is* a second-class berth, Monsieur –'

'Well, then –'

'But it is a lady's berth. There is already a German woman in the compartment – a lady's-maid.'

31

'*Là, là*, that is awkward,' said M. Bouc.

'Do not distress yourself, my friend,' said Poirot. 'I must travel in an ordinary carriage.'

'Not at all. Not at all.' He turned once more to the conductor. 'Everyone has arrived?'

'It is true,' said the man, 'that there is one passenger who has not yet arrived.'

He spoke slowly with hesitation.

'But speak then?'

'No. 7 berth – a second-class. The gentleman has not yet come, and it is four minutes to nine.'

'Who is it?'

'An Englishman,' the conductor consulted his list. 'A M. Harris.'

'A name of good omen,' said Poirot. 'I read my Dickens. M. Harris, he will not arrive.'

'Put Monsieur's luggage in No. 7,' said M. Bouc. 'If this M. Harris arrives we will tell him that he is too late – that berths cannot be retained so long – we will arrange the matter one way or another. What do I care for a M. Harris?'

'As Monsieur pleases,' said the conductor.

He spoke to Poirot's porter, directing him where to go.

Then he stood aside the steps to let Poirot enter the train. '*Tout à fait au bout, Monsieur*,' he called. 'The end compartment but one.'

Poirot passed along the corridor, a somewhat slow progress, as most of the people travelling were standing outside their carriages.

His polite '*Pardons*' were uttered with the regularity of clockwork. At last he reached the compartment indicated. Inside it, reaching up to a suitcase, was the tall young American of the Tokatlian.

He frowned as Poirot entered.

'Excuse me,' he said. 'I think you've made a mistake.' Then, laboriously in French, '*Je crois que vous avez un erreur.*'

Poirot replied in English.

'You are Mr Harris?'

'No, my name is MacQueen. I –'

But at that moment the voice of the Wagon Lit conductor spoke from over Poirot's shoulder. An apologetic, rather breathless voice.

'There is no other berth on the train, Monsieur. The gentleman has to come in here.'

He was hauling up the corridor window as he spoke and began to lift in Poirot's luggage.

Poirot noticed the apology in his tone with some amusement. Doubtless the man had been promised a good tip if he could keep the compartment for the sole use of the other traveller. However, even the most munificent of tips lose their effect when a director of the company is on board and issues his orders.

The conductor emerged from the compartment, having swung the suit-cases up on to the racks.

'*Voilà Monsieur*,' he said. 'All is arranged. Yours is the upper berth, the number 7. We start in one minute.'

He hurried off down the corridor. Poirot re-entered the compartment.

'A phenomenon I have seldom seen,' he said cheerfully. 'A Wagon Lit conductor himself puts up the luggage! It is unheard of!'

His fellow traveller smiled. He had evidently got over his annoyance – had probably decided that it was no good to take the matter other than philosophically.

'The train's remarkably full,' he said.

A whistle blew, there was a long, melancholy cry from the engine. Both men stepped out into the corridor.

Outside a voice shouted.

'*En voiture*.'

'We're off,' said MacQueen.

But they were not quite off. The whistle blew again.

'I say, sir,' said the young man suddenly, 'if you'd rather have the lower berth – easier, and all that – well, that's all right by me.'

'No, no,' protested Poirot. 'I would not deprive you –'

'That's all right –'

'You are too amiable –'

Polite protests on both sides.

'It is for one night only,' explained Poirot. 'At Belgrade –'

'Oh, I see. You're getting out at Belgrade –'

'Not exactly. You see –'

There was a sudden jerk. Both men swung round to the window, looking out at the long, lighted platform as it slid slowly past them.

The Orient Express had started on its three-days' journey across Europe.

Chapter 3

Poirot Refuses a Case

M. Hercule Poirot was a little late in entering the luncheon-car on the following day. He had risen early, breakfasted almost alone, and had spent the morning going over the notes of the case that was recalling him to London. He had seen little of his travelling companion.

M. Bouc, who was already seated, gesticulated a greeting and summoned his friend to the empty place opposite him. Poirot sat down and soon found himself in the favoured position of the table which was served first and with the choicest morsels. The food, too, was unusually good.

It was not till they were eating a delicate cream cheese that M. Bouc allowed his attention to wander to matters other than nourishment. He was at the stage of a meal when one becomes philosophic.

'Ah!' he sighed. 'If I had but the pen of a Balzac! I would depict this scene.'

He waved his hand.

'It is an idea, that,' said Poirot.

'Ah, you agree? It has not been done, I think? And yet – it lends itself to romance, my friend. All around us are people, of all classes, of all nationalities, of all ages. For three days these people, these strangers to one another, are brought together. They sleep and eat under one roof, they cannot get away from each other. At the end of three days they part, they go their several ways, never, perhaps, to see each other again.'

'And yet,' said Poirot, 'suppose an accident –'

'Ah no, my friend –'

'From your point of view it would be regrettable, I agree. But nevertheless let us just for one moment suppose it. Then, perhaps, all these here are linked together – by death.'

'Some more wine,' said M. Bouc, hastily pouring it out. 'You are morbid, *mon cher*. It is, perhaps, the digestion.'

'It is true,' agreed Poirot, 'that the food in Syria was not, perhaps, quite suited to my stomach.'

He sipped his wine. Then, leaning back, he ran his eye thoughtfully round the dining-car. There were thirteen people seated there and, as M. Bouc had said, of all classes and nationalities. He began to study them.

At the table opposite them were three men. They

were, he guessed, single travellers graded and placed there by the unerring judgment of the restaurant attendants. A big, swarthy Italian was picking his teeth with gusto. Opposite him a spare, neat Englishman had the expressionless disapproving face of the well-trained servant. Next to the Englishman was a big American in a loud suit – possibly a commercial traveller.

'You've got to put it over *big*,' he was saying in a loud nasal voice.

The Italian removed his toothpick to gesticulate with it freely.

'Sure,' he said. 'That whatta I say alla de time.'

The Englishman looked out of the window and coughed.

Poirot's eye passed on.

At a small table, sitting very upright, was one of the ugliest old ladies he had ever seen. It was an ugliness of distinction – it fascinated rather than repelled. She sat very upright. Round her neck was a collar of very large pearls which, improbable though it seemed, were real. Her hands were covered with rings. Her sable coat was pushed back on her shoulders. A very small expensive black toque was hideously unbecoming to the yellow, toad-like face beneath it.

She was speaking now to the restaurant attendant in a clear, courteous but completely autocratic tone.

39

'You will be sufficiently amiable to place in my compartment a bottle of mineral water and a large glass of orange juice. You will arrange that I shall have chicken cooked without sauces for dinner this evening – also some boiled fish.'

The attendant replied respectfully that it should be done.

She gave a slight gracious nod of the head and rose. Her glance caught Poirot's and swept over him with the nonchalance of the uninterested aristocrat.

'That is Princess Dragomiroff,' said M. Bouc in a low tone. 'She is a Russian. Her husband realized all this money before the Revolution and invested it abroad. She is extremely rich. A cosmopolitan.'

Poirot nodded. He had heard of Princess Dragomiroff.

'She is a personality,' said M. Bouc. 'Ugly as sin, but she makes herself felt. You agree?'

Poirot agreed.

At another of the large tables Mary Debenham was sitting with two other women. One of them was a tall middle-aged woman in a plaid blouse and tweed skirt. She had a mass of faded yellow hair unbecomingly arranged in a large bun, wore glasses, and had a long, mild, amiable face rather like a sheep. She was listening to the third woman, a stout, pleasant-faced, elderly woman who was talking in a slow clear monotone which showed no signs of pausing for breath or coming to a stop.

' . . . And so my daughter said, "Why," she said "you just can't apply Amurrican methods in this country. It's just natural to the folks here to be indolent," she said. "They just haven't got any hustle in them." But all the same you'd be surprised to know what our college there is doing. They've gotten a fine staff of teachers. I guess there's nothing like education. We've got to apply our Western ideals and teach the East to recognize them. My daughter says –'

The train plunged into a tunnel. The calm monotonous voice was drowned.

At the next table, a small one, sat Colonel Arbuthnot – alone. His gaze was fixed upon the back of Mary Debenham's head. They were not sitting together. Yet it could easily have been managed. Why?

Perhaps, Poirot thought, Mary Debenham had demurred. A governess learns to be careful. Appearances are important. A girl with her living to get has to be discreet.

His glance shifted to the other side of the carriage. At the far end, against the wall, was a middle-aged woman dressed in black with a broad expressionless face. German or Scandinavian, he thought. Probably a German lady's-maid.

After her came a couple leaning forward and talking

41

animatedly together. The man wore English clothes of loose tweed – but he was not English. Though only the back of his head was visible to Poirot, the shape of it and the set of the shoulders betrayed him. A big man, well made. He turned his head suddenly and Poirot saw his profile. A very handsome man of thirty odd with a big fair moustache.

The woman opposite him was a mere girl – twenty at a guess. A tight-fitting little black coat and skirt, white satin blouse, small chic black toque perched at the fashionable outrageous angle. She had a beautiful foreign-looking face, dead white skin, large brown eyes, jet-black hair. She was smoking a cigarette in a long holder. Her manicured hands had deep red nails. She wore one large emerald set in platinum. There was coquetry in her glance and voice.

'*Elle est jolie – et chic*,' murmured Poirot. 'Husband and wife – eh?'

M. Bouc nodded.

'Hungarian Embassy, I believe,' he said. 'A handsome couple.'

There were only two more lunchers – Poirot's fellow traveller MacQueen and his employer Mr Ratchett. The latter sat facing Poirot, and for the second time Poirot studied that unprepossessing face, noting the false benevolence of the brow and the small, cruel eyes.

Doubtless M. Bouc saw a change in his friend's expression.

'It is at your wild animal you look?' he asked.

Poirot nodded.

As his coffee was brought to him, M. Bouc rose to his feet. Having started before Poirot, he had finished some time ago.

'I return to my compartment,' he said. 'Come along presently and converse with me.'

'With pleasure.'

Poirot sipped his coffee and ordered a liqueur. The attendant was passing from table to table with his box of money, accepting payment for bills. The elderly American lady's voice rose shrill and plaintive.

'My daughter said, "Take a book of food tickets and you'll have no trouble – no trouble at all." Now, that isn't so. Seems they have to have a ten per cent. tip, and then there's that bottle of mineral water – and a queer sort of water too. They hadn't got any Evian or Vichy, which seems queer to me.'

'It is – they must – how you say – serve the water of the country,' explained the sheep-faced lady.

'Well, it seems queer to me.' She looked distastefully at the heap of small change on the table in front of her. 'Look at all this peculiar stuff he's given me. Dinars or something. Just a lot of rubbish, it looks. My daughter said –'

Mary Debenham pushed back her chair and left with a slight bow to the other two. Colonel Arbuthnot got up and followed her. Gathering up her despised money, the American lady followed suit, followed by the lady like a sheep. The Hungarians had already departed. The restaurant-car was empty save for Poirot and Ratchett and MacQueen.

Ratchett spoke to his companion, who got up and left the car. Then he rose himself, but instead of following MacQueen he dropped unexpectedly into the seat opposite Poirot.

'Can you oblige me with a light?' he said. His voice was soft – faintly nasal. 'My name is Ratchett.'

Poirot bowed slightly. He slipped his hand into his pocket and produced a matchbox which he handed to the other man, who took it but did not strike a light.

'I think,' he went on, 'that I have the pleasure of speaking to M. Hercule Poirot. Is that so?'

Poirot bowed again.

'You have been correctly informed, Monsieur.'

The detective was conscious of those strange shrewd eyes summing him up before the other spoke again.

'In my country,' he said, 'we come to the point quickly. Mr Poirot, I want you to take on a job for me.'

Hercule Poirot's eyebrows went up a trifle.

'My *clientèle*, Monsieur, is limited nowadays. I undertake very few cases.'

'Why, naturally, I understand that. But this, Mr Poirot, means big money.' He repeated again in his soft, persuasive voice, 'Big money.'

Hercule Poirot was silent a minute or two, then he said:

'What is it you wish me to do for you, M. – er – Ratchett?'

'Mr Poirot, I am a rich man – a very rich man. Men in that position have enemies. I have an enemy.'

'Only one enemy?'

'Just what do you mean by that question?' asked Ratchett sharply.

'Monsieur, in my experience when a man is in a position to have, as you say, enemies, then it does not usually resolve itself into one enemy only.'

Ratchett seemed relieved by Poirot's answer. He said quickly:

'Why, yes, I appreciate that point. Enemy or enemies – it doesn't matter. What does matter is my safety.'

'Safety?'

'My life has been threatened, Mr Poirot. Now, I'm a man who can take pretty good care of himself.' From the pocket of his coat his hand brought a small automatic into sight for a moment. He continued grimly. 'I don't think I'm the kind of man to be caught napping. But as I look at it I might as well make assurance doubly sure. I fancy you're the man for my money, Mr Poirot. And remember – *big* money.'

Poirot looked at him thoughtfully for some minutes. His face was completely expressionless. The other could have had no clue as to what thoughts were passing in that mind.

'I regret, Monsieur,' he said at length. 'I cannot oblige you.'

The other looked at him shrewdly.

'Name your figure, then,' he said.

Poirot shook his head.

'You do not understand, Monsieur. I have been very fortunate in my profession. I have made enough money to satisfy both my needs and my caprices. I take now only such cases as – interest me.'

'You've got a pretty good nerve,' said Ratchett. 'Will twenty thousand dollars tempt you?'

'It will not.'

'If you're holding out for more, you won't get it. I know what a thing's worth to me.'

'I also – M. Ratchett.'

'What's wrong with my proposition?'

Poirot rose.

'If you will forgive me for being personal – I do not like your face, M. Ratchett,' he said.

And with that he left the restaurant car.

Chapter 4

A Cry in the Night

The Simplon Orient Express arrived at Belgrade at a quarter to nine that evening. It was not due to depart again until 9.15, so Poirot descended to the platform. He did not, however, remain there long. The cold was bitter and though the platform itself was protected, heavy snow was falling outside. He returned to his compartment. The conductor, who was on the platform stamping his feet and waving his arms to keep warm, spoke to him.

'Your valises have been moved, Monsieur, to the compartment No. 1, the compartment of M. Bouc.'

'But where is M. Bouc, then?'

'He has moved into the coach from Athens which has just been put on.'

Poirot went in search of his friend. M. Bouc waved his protestations aside.

'It is nothing. It is nothing. It is more convenient

47

like this. You are going through to England, so it is better that you should stay in the through coach to Calais. Me, I am very well here. It is most peaceful. This coach is empty save for myself and one little Greek doctor. Ah! my friend, what a night! They say there has not been so much snow for years. Let us hope we shall not be held up. I am not too happy about it, I can tell you.'

At 9.15 punctually the train pulled out of the station, and shortly afterwards Poirot got up, said good-night to his friend and made his way along the corridor back into his own coach which was in front next to the dining-car.

On this, the second day of the journey, barriers were breaking down. Colonel Arbuthnot was standing at the door of his compartment talking to MacQueen.

MacQueen broke off something he was saying when he saw Poirot. He looked very surprised.

'Why,' he cried, 'I thought you'd left us. You said you were getting off at Belgrade.'

'You misunderstood me,' said Poirot, smiling. 'I remember now, the train started from Stamboul just as we were talking about it.'

'But, man, your baggage – it's gone.'

'It has been moved into another compartment – that is all.'

'Oh, I see.'

He resumed his conversation with Arbuthnot and Poirot passed on down the corridor.

Two doors from his own compartment, the elderly American lady, Mrs Hubbard, was standing talking to the sheep-like lady who was a Swede. Mrs Hubbard was pressing a magazine on the other.

'No, do take it, my dear,' she said. 'I've got plenty other things to read. My, isn't the cold something frightful?' She nodded amicably to Poirot.

'You are most kind,' said the Swedish lady.

'Not at all. I hope you'll sleep well and that your head will be better in the morning.'

'It is the cold only. I make now myself a cup of tea.'

'Have you got some aspirin? Are you sure, now? I've got plenty. Well, good-night, my dear.'

She turned to Poirot conversationally as the other woman departed.

'Poor creature, she's a Swede. As far as I can make out, she's a kind of missionary – a teaching one. A nice creature, but doesn't talk much English. She was *most* interested in what I told her about my daughter.'

Poirot, by now, knew all about Mrs Hubbard's daughter. Everyone on the train who could understand English did! How she and her husband were on the staff of a big American college in Smyrna and how this was Mrs Hubbard's first journey to the East, and

49

what she thought of the Turks and their slipshod ways and the condition of their roads.

The door next to them opened and the thin, pale manservant stepped out. Inside Poirot caught a glimpse of Mr Ratchett sitting up in bed. He saw Poirot and his face changed, darkening with anger. Then the door was shut.

Mrs Hubbard drew Poirot a little aside.

'You know, I'm dead scared of that man. Oh, not the valet – the other – his master. Master, indeed! There's something *wrong* about that man. My daughter always says I'm very intuitive. "When Momma gets a hunch, she's dead right," that's what my daughter says. And I've got a hunch about that man. He's next door to me, and I don't like it. I put my grips against the communicating door last night. I thought I heard him trying the handle. Do you know, I shouldn't be surprised if that man turns out to be a murderer – one of these train robbers you read about. I dare say I'm foolish, but there it is. I'm downright scared of the man! My daughter said I'd have an easy journey, but somehow I don't feel happy about it. It may be foolish, but I feel anything might happen. Anything at all. And how that nice young fellow can bear to be his secretary I can't think.'

Colonel Arbuthnot and MacQueen were coming towards them down the corridor.

'Come into my carriage,' MacQueen was saying. 'It isn't made up for the night yet. Now what I want to get right about your policy in India is this –'

The men passed and went on down the corridor to MacQueen's carriage.

Mrs Hubbard said good-night to Poirot.

'I guess I'll go right to bed and read,' she said. 'Good-night.'

'Good-night, Madame.'

Poirot passed into his own compartment, which was the next one beyond Ratchett's. He undressed and got into bed, read for about half an hour and then turned out the light.

He awoke some hours later, and awoke with a start. He knew what it was that had wakened him – a loud groan, almost a cry, somewhere close at hand. At the same moment the ting of a bell sounded sharply.

Poirot sat up and switched on the light. He noticed that the train was at a standstill – presumably at a station.

That cry had startled him. He remembered that it was Ratchett who had the next compartment. He got out of bed and opened the door just as the Wagon Lit conductor came hurrying along the corridor and knocked on Ratchett's door. Poirot kept his door open a crack and watched. The conductor tapped a second time. A bell rang and a light showed over another

51

door farther down. The conductor glanced over his shoulder.

At the same moment a voice from within the next-door compartment called out:

'*Ce n'est rien. Je me suis trompé.*'

'*Bien, Monsieur.*' The conductor scurried off again, to knock at the door where the light was showing.

Poirot returned to bed, his mind relieved, and switched off the light. He glanced at his watch. It was just twenty-three minutes to one.

Chapter 5

The Crime

He found it difficult to go to sleep again at once. For one thing, he missed the motion of the train. If it *was* a station outside it was curiously quiet. By contrast, the noises on the train seemed unusually loud. He could hear Ratchett moving about next door – a click as he pulled down the washbasin, the sound of the tap running, a splashing noise, then another click as the basin shut to again. Footsteps passed up the corridor outside, the shuffling footsteps of someone in bedroom slippers.

Hercule Poirot lay awake staring at the ceiling. Why was the station outside so silent? His throat felt dry. He had forgotten to ask for his usual bottle of mineral water. He looked at his watch again. Just after a quarter-past one. He would ring for the conductor and ask him for some mineral water. His finger went out to the bell, but he paused as in the stillness he heard a ting. The man couldn't answer every bell at once.

Ting . . . ting . . . ting . . .

It sounded again and again. Where was the man? Somebody was getting impatient.

Ting . . .

Whoever it was was keeping their finger solidly on the push.

Suddenly with a rush, his footsteps echoing up the aisle, the man came. He knocked at a door not far from Poirot's own.

Then came voices – the conductor's, deferential, apologetic, and a woman's – insistent and voluble.

Mrs Hubbard.

Poirot smiled to himself.

The altercation – if it was one – went on for some time. Its proportions were ninety per cent. of Mrs Hubbard's to a soothing ten per cent. of the conductor's. Finally the matter seemed to be adjusted. Poirot heard distinctly:

'*Bonne nuit*, Madame,' and a closing door.

He pressed his own finger on the bell.

The conductor arrived promptly. He looked hot and worried.

'*De l'eau minerale, s'il vous plait.*'

'*Bien, Monsieur.*' Perhaps a twinkle in Poirot's eye led him to unburden himself.

'*La Dame Americaine* –'

'Yes?'

He wiped his forehead.

'Imagine to yourself the time I have had with her! She insists – but *insists* – that there is a man in her compartment! Figure to yourself, Monsieur. In a space of this size.' He swept a hand round. 'Where would he conceal himself? I argue with her. I point out that it is impossible. She insists. She woke up and there was a man there. And how, I ask, did he get out and leave the door bolted behind him? But she will not listen to reason. As though, there were not enough to worry us already. This snow –'

'Snow?'

'But yes, Monsieur. Monsieur has not noticed? The train has stopped. We have run into a snowdrift. Heaven knows how long we shall be here. I remember once being snowed up for seven days.'

'Where are we?'

'Between Vincovi and Brod.'

'*Là là,*' said Poirot vexedly.

The man withdrew and returned with the water.

'*Bon soir, Monsieur.*'

Poirot drank a glass of water and composed himself to sleep.

He was just dropping off when something again

woke him. This time it was as though something heavy had fallen with a thud against the door.

He sprang up, opened it and looked out. Nothing. But to his right some way down the corridor a woman wrapped in a scarlet kimono was retreating from him. At the other end, sitting on his little seat, the conductor was entering up figures on large sheets of paper. Everything was deathly quiet.

'Decidedly I suffer from the nerves,' said Poirot and retired to bed again. This time he slept till morning.

When he awoke the train was still at a standstill. He raised a blind and looked out. Heavy banks of snow surrounded the train.

He glanced at his watch and saw that it was past nine o'clock.

At a quarter to ten, neat, spruce, and dandified as ever, he made his way to the restaurant-car, where a chorus of woe was going on.

Any barriers there might have been between the passengers had now quite broken down. All were united by a common misfortune. Mrs Hubbard was loudest in her lamentations.

'My daughter said it would be the easiest way in the world. Just sit in the train until I got to Parrus. And now we may be here for days and days,' she wailed. 'And my boat sails the day after tomorrow.

How am I going to catch it now? Why, I can't even wire to cancel my passage. I feel too mad to talk about it.'

The Italian said that he had urgent business himself in Milan. The large American said that that was 'too bad, Ma'am,' and soothingly expressed a hope that the train might make up time.

'My sister – her children wait me,' said the Swedish lady and wept. 'I get no word to them. What they think? They will say bad things have happen to me.'

'How long shall we be here?' demanded Mary Debenham. 'Doesn't anybody *know*?'

Her voice sounded impatient, but Poirot noted that there were no signs of that almost feverish anxiety which she had displayed during the check to the Taurus Express.

Mrs Hubbard was off again.

'There isn't anybody knows a thing on this train. And nobody's trying to do anything. Just a pack of useless foreigners. Why, if this were at home, there'd be someone at least *trying* to do something.'

Arbuthnot turned to Poirot and spoke in careful British French.

'*Vous êtes un directeur de la ligne, je crois, Monsieur. Vous pouvez nous dire –*'

Smiling Poirot corrected him.

'No, no,' he said in English. 'It is not I. You confound me with my friend M. Bouc.'

'Oh! I'm sorry.'

'Not at all. It is most natural. I am now in the compartment that he had formerly.'

M. Bouc was not present in the restaurant-car. Poirot looked about to notice who else was absent.

Princess Dragomiroff was missing and the Hungarian couple. Also Ratchett, his valet, and the German lady's-maid.

The Swedish lady wiped her eyes.

'I am foolish,' she said. 'I am baby to cry. All for the best, whatever happen.'

This Christian spirit, however, was far from being shared.

'That's all very well,' said MacQueen restlessly. 'We may be here for days.'

'What is this country anyway?' demanded Mrs Hubbard tearfully.

On being told it was Yugo-Slavia she said:

'Oh! one of these Balkan things. What can you expect?'

'You are the only patient one, Mademoiselle,' said Poirot to Miss Debenham.

She shrugged her shoulders slightly.

'What can one do?'

'You are a philosopher, Mademoiselle.'

'That implies a detached attitude. I think my attitude is more selfish. I have learned to save myself useless emotion.'

She was not even looking at him. Her gaze went past him, out of the window to where the snow lay in heavy masses.

'You are a strong character, Mademoiselle,' said Poirot gently. 'You are, I think, the strongest character amongst us.'

'Oh, no. No, indeed. I know one far far stronger than I am.'

'And that is –?'

She seemed suddenly to come to herself, to realize that she was talking to a stranger and a foreigner with whom, until this morning, she had only exchanged half a dozen sentences.

She laughed a polite but estranging laugh.

'Well – that old lady, for instance. You have probably noticed her. A very ugly old lady, but rather fascinating. She has only to lift a little finger and ask for something in a polite voice – and the whole train runs.'

'It runs also for my friend M. Bouc,' said Poirot. 'But that is because he is a director of the line, not because he has a masterful character.'

Mary Debenham smiled.

The morning wore away. Several people, Poirot

amongst them, remained in the dining-car. The communal life was felt, at the moment, to pass the time better. He heard a good deal more about Mrs Hubbard's daughter and he heard the lifelong habits of Mr Hubbard, deceased, from his rising in the morning and commencing breakfast with a cereal to his final rest at night in the bed-socks that Mrs Hubbard herself had been in the habit of knitting for him.

It was when he was listening to a confused account of the missionary aims of the Swedish lady that one of the Wagon Lit conductors came into the car and stood at his elbow.

'*Pardon, Monsieur.*'

'Yes?'

'The compliments of M. Bouc, and he would be glad if you would be so kind as to come to him for a few minutes.'

Poirot rose, uttered excuses to the Swedish lady and followed the man out of the dining-car.

It was not his own conductor, but a big fair man.

He followed his guide down the corridor of his own carriage and along the corridor of the next one. The man tapped at a door, then stood aside to let Poirot enter.

The compartment was not M. Bouc's own. It was a second-class one – chosen presumably because of its slightly larger size. It certainly gave the impression of being crowded.

M. Bouc himself was sitting on the small seat in the opposite corner. In the corner next the window facing him was a small, dark man looking out at the snow. Standing up and quite preventing Poirot from advancing any farther was a big man in blue uniform (the *chef de train*) and his own Wagon Lit conductor.

'Ah, my good friend,' cried M. Bouc. 'Come in. We have need of you.'

The little man in the window shifted along the seat, Poirot squeezed past the other two men and sat down facing his friend.

The expression on M. Bouc's face gave him, as he would have expressed it, furiously to think. It was clear that something out of the common had happened.

'What has occurred?' he asked.

'You may well ask that. First this snow – this stoppage. And now –'

He paused – and a sort of strangled gasp came from the Wagon Lit conductor.

'And now what?'

'*And now a passenger lies dead in his berth – stabbed.*'

M. Bouc spoke with a kind of calm desperation.

'A passenger? Which passenger?'

Agatha Christie

'An American. A man called – called –' he consulted some notes in front of him. 'Ratchett – that is right – Ratchett?'

'Yes, Monsieur,' the Wagon Lit man gulped.

Poirot looked at him. He was as white as chalk.

'You had better let that man sit down,' he said. 'He may faint otherwise.'

The *chef de train* moved slightly and the Wagon Lit man sank down in the corner and buried his face in his hands.

'Brr!' said Poirot. 'This is serious!'

'Certainly it is serious. To begin with, a murder – that by itself is a calamity of the first water. But not only that, the circumstances are unusual. Here we are, brought to a standstill. We may be here for hours – and not only hours – days! Another circumstance. Passing through most countries we have the police of that country on the train. But in Yugoslavia – no. You comprehend?'

'It is a position of great difficulty,' said Poirot.

'There is worse to come. Dr Constantine – I forgot, I have not introduced you – Dr Constantine, M. Poirot.'

The little dark man bowed and Poirot returned it.

'Dr Constantine is of the opinion that death occurred at about 1 a.m.'

'It is difficult to say exactly in these matters,' said

the doctor, 'but I think I can say definitely that death occurred between midnight and two in the morning.'

'When was this M. Ratchett last seen alive?' asked Poirot.

'He is known to have been alive at about twenty minutes to one, when he spoke to the conductor,' said M. Bouc.

'That is quite correct,' said Poirot. 'I myself heard what passed. That is the last thing known?'

'Yes.'

Poirot turned toward the doctor, who continued?

'The window of M. Ratchett's compartment was found wide open, leading one to suppose that the murderer escaped that way. But in my opinion that open window is a blind. Anyone departing that way would have left distinct traces in the snow. There were none.'

'The crime was discovered – when?' asked Poirot.

'Michel!'

The Wagon Lit conductor sat up. His face still looked pale and frightened.

'Tell this gentleman exactly what occurred,' ordered M. Bouc.

The man spoke somewhat jerkily.

'The valet of this M. Ratchett, he tapped several times at the door this morning. There was no answer.

Then, half an hour ago, the restaurant-car attendant came. He wanted to know if Monsieur was taking *déjeuner*. It was eleven o'clock, you comprehend.

'I open the door for him with my key. But there is a chain, too, and that is fastened. There is no answer and it is very still in there, and cold – but cold. With the window open and snow drifting in. I thought the gentleman had had a fit, perhaps. I got the *chef de train*. We broke the chain and went in. He was – *Ah! c'était terrible!*'

He buried his face in his hands again.

'The door was locked and chained on the inside,' said Poirot thoughtfully. 'It was not suicide – eh?'

The Greek doctor gave a sardonic laugh.

'Does a man who commits suicide stab himself in ten – twelve – fifteen places?' he asked.

Poirot's eyes opened.

'That is great ferocity,' he said.

'It is a woman,' said the *chef de train*, speaking for the first time. 'Depend upon it, it was a woman. Only a woman would stab like that.'

Dr Constantine screwed up his face thoughtfully.

'She must have been a very strong woman,' he said. 'It is not my desire to speak technically – that is only confusing – but I can assure you that one or two of the blows were delivered with such force as to drive them through hard belts of bone and muscle.'

'It was not, clearly, a scientific crime,' said Poirot.

'It was most unscientific,' said Dr Constantine. 'The blows seem to have been delivered haphazard and at random. Some have glanced off, doing hardly any damage. It is as though somebody had shut their eyes and then in a frenzy struck blindly again and again.'

'*C'est une femme*,' said the *chef de train* again. 'Women are like that. When they are enraged they have great strength.' He nodded so sagely that everyone suspected a personal experience of his own.

'I have, perhaps, something to contribute to your store of knowledge,' said Poirot. 'M. Ratchett spoke to me yesterday. He told me, as far as I was able to understand him, that he was in danger of his life.'

'"Bumped off" – that is the American expression, is it not?' said M. Bouc. 'Then it is not a woman. It is a "Gangster" or a "gunman."'

The *chef de train* looked pained at his theory having come to naught.

'If so,' said Poirot, 'it seems to have been done very amateurishly.'

His tone expressed professional disapproval.

'There is a large American on the train,' said M. Bouc, pursuing his idea – 'a common-looking man with terrible clothes. He chews the gum which I believe is not done in good circles. You know whom I mean?'

The Wagon Lit conductor to whom he had appealed nodded.

'*Oui*, Monsieur, the No. 16. But it cannot have been he. I should have seen him enter or leave the compartment.'

'You might not. You might not. But we will go into that presently. The question is, what to do?' He looked at Poirot.

Poirot looked back at him.

'Come, my friend,' said M. Bouc. 'You comprehend what I am about to ask of you. I know your powers. Take command of this investigation! No, no, do not refuse. See, to us it is serious – I speak for the Compagnie Internationale des Wagons Lits. By the time the Yugo-Slavian police arrive, how simple if we can present them with the solution! Otherwise delays, annoyances, a million and one inconveniences. Perhaps, who knows, serious annoyance to innocent persons. Instead – *you* solve the mystery! We say, "A murder has occurred – *this* is the criminal!"'

'And suppose I do not solve it?'

'Ah! *mon cher.*' M. Bouc's voice became positively caressing. 'I know your reputation. I know something of your methods. This is the ideal case for you. To look up the antecedents of all these people, to discover their *bona fides* – all that takes time and endless inconvenience. But have I not heard you say often that to solve a case a man has only to lie back in his chair and think? Do that. Interview the passengers on the train, view the body, examine what clues there are and then – well, I have faith in you! I am assured that it is no idle boast of yours. Lie back and think – use (as I have heard you say so often) the little grey cells of the mind – and you will *know!*'

He leaned forward, looking affectionately at his friend.

'Your faith touches me, my friend,' said Poirot emotionally. 'As you say, this cannot be a difficult case. I myself, last night – but we will not speak of that now. In truth, this problem intrigues me. I was reflecting, not half an hour ago, that many hours of boredom lay ahead whilst we are stuck here. And now – a problem lies ready to my hand.'

'You accept then?' said M. Bouc eagerly.

'*C'est entendu.* You place the matter in my hands.'

'Good – we are all at your service.'

'To begin with, I should like a plan of the Istanbul-Calais coach, with a note of the people who occupied the several compartments, and I should also like to see their passports and their tickets.'

'Michel will get you those.'

The Wagon Lit conductor left the compartment.

'What other passengers are there on the train?' asked Poirot.

'In this coach Dr Constantine and I are the only travellers. In the coach from Bucharest is an old gentleman with a lame leg. He is well known to the conductor. Beyond that are the ordinary carriages, but these do not concern us, since they were locked after dinner had been served last night. Forward of the Istanbul-Calais coach there is only the dining-car.'

'Then it seems,' said Poirot slowly, 'as though we must look for our murderer in the Istanbul-Calais coach.' He turned to the doctor. 'That is what you were hinting, I think?'

The Greek nodded.

'At half an hour after midnight we ran into the snow-drift. No one can have left the train since then.'

M. Bouc said solemnly.

'*The murderer is with us – on the train now . . .*'

Chapter 6

A Woman?

'First of all,' said Poirot, 'I should like a word or two with young M. MacQueen. He may be able to give us valuable information.'

'Certainly,' said M. Bouc.

He turned to the *chef de train*.

'Get M. MacQueen to come here.'

The *chef de train* left the carriage.

The conductor returned with a bundle of passports and tickets. M. Bouc took them from him.

'Thank you, Michel. It would be best now, I think, if you were to go back to your post. We will take your evidence formally later.'

'Very good, Monsieur.'

Michel in his turn left the carriage.

'After we have seen young MacQueen,' said Poirot, 'perhaps M. le docteur will come with me to the dead man's carriage.'

Agatha Christie

'Certainly.'

'After we have finished there –'

But at this moment the *chef de train* returned with Hector MacQueen.

M. Bouc rose.

'We are a little cramped here,' he said pleasantly. 'Take my seat, M. MacQueen. M. Poirot will sit opposite you – so.'

He turned to the *chef de train*.

'Clear all the people out of the restaurant-car,' he said, 'and let it be left free for M. Poirot. You will conduct your interviews there, *mon cher*?'

'It would be the most convenient, yes,' agreed Poirot.

MacQueen had stood looking from one to the other, not quite following the rapid flow of French.

'*Qu'est ce qu'il y a?*' he began laboriously. '*Pourquoi –?*'

With a vigorous gesture Poirot motioned him to the seat in the corner. He took it and began once more.

'*Pourquoi –?*' then, checking himself and relapsing into his own tongue, 'What's up on the train? Has anything happened?'

He looked from one man to another.

Poirot nodded.

'Exactly. Something has happened. Prepare yourself for a shock. *Your employer, M. Ratchett, is dead!*'

MacQueen's mouth pursed itself in a whistle. Except that his eyes grew a shade brighter, he showed no signs of shock or distress.

'So they got him after all,' he said.

'What exactly do you mean by that phrase, M. MacQueen?' MacQueen hesitated.

'You are assuming,' said Poirot, 'that M. Ratchett was murdered?'

'Wasn't he?' This time MacQueen did show surprise. 'Why, yes,' he said slowly. 'That's just what I did think. Do you mean he just died in his sleep? Why, the old man was as tough as – as tough –'

He stopped, at a loss for a simile.

'No, no,' said Poirot. 'Your assumption was quite right. Mr Ratchett was murdered. Stabbed. But I should like to know why you were so sure it *was* murder, and not just – death.'

MacQueen hesitated.

'I must get this clear,' he said. 'Who exactly are you? And where do you come in?'

'I represent the Compagnie Internationale des Wagons Lits.' He paused, then added, 'I am a detective. My name is Hercule Poirot.'

If he expected an effect he did not get one. MacQueen said merely, 'Oh, yes?' and waited for him to go on.

'You know the name, perhaps.'

'Why, it does seem kind of familiar – only I always thought it was a woman's dressmaker.'

Hercule Poirot looked at him with distaste.

'It is incredible!' he said.

'What's incredible?'

'Nothing. Let us advance with the matter in hand. I want you to tell me, M. MacQueen, all that you know about the dead man. You were not related to him?'

'No. I am – was – his secretary.'

'For how long have you held that post?'

'Just over a year.'

'Please give me all the information you can.'

'Well, I met Mr Ratchett just over a year ago when I was in Persia –'

Poirot interrupted.

'What were you doing there?'

'I had come over from New York to look into an oil concession. I don't suppose you want to hear all about that. My friends and I had been let in rather badly over it. Mr Ratchett was in the same hotel. He had just had a row with his secretary. He offered me the job and I took it. I was at a loose end, and glad to find a well-paid job ready made, as it were.'

'And since then?'

'We've travelled about. Mr Ratchett wanted to see the world. He was hampered by knowing no languages. I acted more as a courier than as a secretary. It was a pleasant life.'

'Now tell me as much as you can about your employer.'

The young man shrugged his shoulders. A perplexed expression passed over his face.

'That's not so easy.'

'What was his full name?'

'Samuel Edward Ratchett.'

'He was an American citizen?'

'Yes.'

'What part of America did he come from?'

'I don't know.'

'Well, tell me what you do know.'

'The actual truth is, Mr Poirot, that I know nothing at all! Mr Ratchett never spoke of himself, or of his life in America.'

'Why do you think that was?'

'I don't know. I imagined that he might have been ashamed of his beginnings. Some men are.'

'Does that strike you as a satisfactory solution?'

'Frankly, it doesn't.'

'Has he any relations?'

'He never mentioned any.'

Poirot pressed the point.

'You must have formed *some* theory, M. MacQueen.'

'Well, yes, I did. For one thing, I don't believe

Ratchett was his real name. I think he left America definitely in order to escape someone or something. I think he was successful – until a few weeks ago.'

'And then?'

'He began to get letters – threatening letters.'

'Did you see them?'

'Yes. It was my business to attend to his correspondence. The first letter came a fortnight ago.'

'Were these letters destroyed?'

'No, I think I've got a couple still in my files – one I know Ratchett tore up in a rage. Shall I get them for you?'

'If you would be so good.'

MacQueen left the compartment. He returned a few minutes later and laid down two sheets of rather dirty notepaper before Poirot.

The first letter ran as follows:

'Thought you'd doublecross us and get away with it, did you? Not on your life. We're out to GET you, Ratchett, and we WILL get you!'

There was no signature.

With no comment beyond raised eyebrows, Poirot picked up the second letter.

'We're going to take you for a ride, Ratchett. Some time soon. We're going to GET you, see?'

Poirot laid the letter down.

'The style is monotonous!' he said. 'More so than the handwriting.'

MacQueen stared at him.

'You would not observe,' said Poirot pleasantly. 'It requires the eye of one used to such things. This letter was not written by one person, M. MacQueen. Two or more persons wrote it – each writing a letter of a word at a time. Also, the letters are printed. That makes the task of identifying the handwriting much more difficult.'

He paused, then said:

'Did you know that M. Ratchett had applied for help to me?'

'To *you*?'

MacQueen's astonished tone told Poirot quite certainly that the young man had not known of it. He nodded.

'Yes. He was alarmed. Tell me, how did he act when he received the first letter?'

MacQueen hesitated.

'It's difficult to say. He – he – passed it off with a laugh in that quiet way of his. But somehow' – he gave a slight shiver – 'I felt that there was a good deal going on underneath the quietness.'

Poirot nodded. Then he asked an unexpected question.

'Mr MacQueen, will you tell me, quite honestly, exactly how you regarded your employer? Did you like him?'

Hector MacQueen took a moment or two before replying.

'No,' he said at last. 'I did not.'

'Why?'

'I can't exactly say. He was always quite pleasant in his manner.' He paused, then said, 'I'll tell you the truth, Mr Poirot. I disliked and distrusted him. He was, I am sure, a cruel and a dangerous man. I must admit, though, that I have no reasons to advance for my opinion.'

'Thank you, M. MacQueen. One further question – when did you last see M. Ratchett alive?'

'Last evening about' – he thought for a minute – 'ten o'clock, I should say. I went into his compartment to take down some memoranda from him.'

'On what subject?'

'Some tiles and antique pottery that he bought in Persia. What was delivered was not what he had purchased. There has been a long, vexatious correspondence on the subject.'

'And that was the last time M. Ratchett was seen alive?'

'Yes, I suppose so.'

'Do you know when M. Ratchett received the last threatening letter?'

'On the morning of the day we left Constantinople.'

'There is one more question I must ask you, M. MacQueen: were you on good terms with your employer?'

The young man's eyes twinkled suddenly.

'This is where I'm supposed to go all goosefleshy down the back. In the words of a best seller, "You've nothing on me." Ratchett and I were on perfectly good terms.'

'Perhaps, M. MacQueen, you will give me your full name and your address in America.'

MacQueen gave his name – Hector Willard MacQueen, and an address in New York.

Poirot leaned back against the cushions.

'That is all for the present, M. MacQueen,' he said. 'I should be obliged if you would keep the matter of M. Ratchett's death to yourself for a little time.'

'His valet, Masterman, will have to know.'

'He probably knows already,' said Poirot dryly. 'If so try to get him to hold his tongue.'

'That oughtn't to be difficult. He's a Britisher, and does what he calls "Keeps himself to himself." He's a low opinion of Americans and no opinion at all of any other nationality.'

'Thank you, M. MacQueen.'

The American left the carriage.

'Well?' demanded M. Bouc. 'You believe what he says, this young man?'

'He seems honest and straightforward. He did not pretend to any affection for his employer as he probably would have done had he been involved in any way. It is true M. Ratchett did not tell him that he had tried to enlist my services and failed, but I do not think that is really a suspicious circumstance. I fancy M. Ratchett was a gentleman who kept his own counsel on every possible occasion.'

'So you pronounce one person at least innocent of the crime,' said M. Bouc jovially.

Poirot cast on him a look of reproach.

'Me, I suspect everybody till the last minute,' he said. 'All the same, I must admit that I cannot see this sober, long-headed MacQueen losing his head and stabbing his victim twelve or fourteen times. It is not in accord with his psychology – not at all.'

'No,' said Mr Bouc thoughtfully. 'That is the act of a man driven almost crazy with a frenzied hate – it suggests more the Latin temperament. Or else it suggests, as our friend the *chef de train* insisted, a woman.'

Chapter 7
The Body

Followed by Dr Constantine, Poirot made his way to the next coach and the compartment occupied by the murdered man. The conductor came and unlocked the door for them with his key.

The two men passed inside. Poirot turned inquiringly to his companion.

'How much has been disarranged in this compartment?'

'Nothing has been touched. I was careful not to move the body in making my examination.'

Poirot nodded. He looked round him.

The first thing that struck the senses was the intense cold. The window was pushed down as far as it would go and the blind was drawn up.

'Brrr,' observed Poirot.

The other smiled appreciatively.

'I did not like to close it,' he said.

Poirot examined the window carefully.

'You are right,' he announced. 'Nobody left the carriage this way. Possibly the open window was intended to suggest the fact, but, if so, the snow has defeated the murderer's object.'

He examined the frame of the window carefully. Taking a small case from his pocket he blew a little powder over it.

'No fingerprints at all,' he said. 'That means it has been wiped. Well, if there had been fingerprints it would have told us very little. They would have been those of M. Ratchett or his valet or the conductor. Criminals do not make mistakes of that kind nowadays.

'And that being so,' he added cheerfully, 'we might as well shut the window. Positively it is the cold storage in here!'

He suited the action to the word and then turned his attention for the first time to the motionless figure lying in the bunk.

Ratchett lay on his back. His pyjama jacket, stained with rusty patches, had been unbuttoned and thrown back.

'I had to see the nature of the wounds, you see,' explained the doctor.

Poirot nodded. He bent over the body. Finally he straightened himself with a slight grimace.

'It is not pretty,' he said. 'Someone must have stood there and stabbed him again and again. How many wounds are there exactly?'

'I make it twelve. One or two are so slight as to be practically scratches. On the other hand, at least three would be capable of causing death.'

Something in the doctor's tone caught Poirot's attention. He looked at him sharply. The little Greek was standing staring down at the body with a puzzled frown.

'Something strikes you as odd, does it not?' he asked gently. 'Speak, my friend. There is something here that puzzles you?'

'You are right,' acknowledged the other.

'What is it?'

'You see, these two wounds – here and here,' – he pointed. 'They are deep, each cut must have severed blood-vessels – and yet – the edges do not gape. They have not bled as one would have expected.'

'Which suggests?'

'That the man was already dead – some little time dead – when they were delivered. But that is surely absurd.'

'It would seem so,' said Poirot thoughtfully. 'Unless our murderer figured to himself that he had not accomplished his job properly and came back to make quite sure; but that is manifestly absurd! Anything else?'

'Well, just one thing.'

'And that?'

'You see this wound here – under the right arm – near the right shoulder. Take this pencil of mine. Could you deliver such a blow?'

Poirot raised his hand.

'*Précisément*,' he said. 'I see. With the *right* hand it is exceedingly difficult – almost impossible. One would have to strike backhanded, as it were. But if the blow were struck with the *left* hand –'

'Exactly, M. Poirot. That blow was almost certainly struck with the *left* hand.'

'So that our murderer is left-handed? No, it is more difficult than that, is it not?'

'As you say, M. Poirot. Some of these other blows are just as obviously right-handed.'

'Two people. We are back at two people again,' murmured the detective. He asked abruptly:

'Was the electric light on?'

'It is difficult to say. You see it is turned off by the conductor every morning about ten o'clock.'

'The switches will tell us,' said Poirot.

He examined the switch of the top light and also the roll back bed-head light. The former was turned off. The latter was closed.

'*Eh bien*,' he said thoughtfully. 'We have here a hypothesis of the First and Second Murderer, as the

82

great Shakespeare would put it. The First Murderer
stabbed his victim and left the compartment, turning
off the light. The Second Murderer came in in the
dark, did not see that his or her work had been done
and stabbed at least twice at a dead body. *Que pensez
vous de ça?*'

'Magnificent,' said the little doctor with enthusi-
asm.

The other's eyes twinkled.

'You think so? I am glad. It sounded to me a little
like the nonsense.'

'What other explanation can there be?'

'That is just what I am asking myself. Have we
here a coincidence or what? Are there any other
inconsistencies, such as would point to two people
being concerned?'

'I think I can say yes. Some of these blows, as I have
already said, point to a weakness – a lack of strength
or a lack of determination. They are feeble glancing
blows. But this one here – and this one –' Again he
pointed. 'Great strength was needed for those blows.
They have penetrated the muscle.'

'They were, in your opinion, delivered by a man?'

'Most certainly.'

'They could not have been delivered by a woman?'

'A young, vigorous, athletic woman might have

struck them, especially if she were in the grip of a strong emotion, but it is in my opinion highly unlikely.'

Poirot was silent a moment or two.

The other said anxiously.

'You understand my point?'

'Perfectly,' said Poirot. 'The matter begins to clear itself up wonderfully! The murderer was a man of great strength, he was feeble, it was a woman, it was a right-handed person, it was a left-handed person – *Ah! c'est rigolo, tout ça!*'

He spoke with sudden anger.

'And the victim – what does he do in all this? Does he cry out? Does he struggle? Does he defend himself?'

He slipped his hand under the pillow and drew out the automatic pistol which Ratchett had shown him the day before.

'Fully loaded, you see,' he said.

They looked round them. Ratchett's day clothing was hanging from the hooks on the wall. On the small table formed by the lid of the washing basin were various objects – false teeth in a glass of water; another glass, empty; a bottle of mineral water, a large flask and an ash-tray containing the butt of a cigar and some charred fragments of paper; also two burnt matches.

The doctor picked up the empty glass and sniffed it.

'Here is the explanation of the victim's inertia,' he said quietly.

'Drugged?'

'Yes.'

Poirot nodded. He picked up the two matches and scrutinized them carefully.

'You have a clue then?' demanded the little doctor eagerly.

'Those two matches are of a different shape,' said Poirot. 'One is flatter than the other. You see?'

'It is the kind you get on a train,' said the doctor, 'in paper covers.'

Poirot was feeling in the pockets of Ratchett's clothing. Presently he pulled out a box of matches. He compared them carefully.

'The rounder one is a match struck by Mr Ratchett,' he said. 'Let us see if he had also the flatter kind.'

But a further search showed no other matches.

Poirot's eyes were darting about the compartment. They were bright and sharp like a bird's. One felt that nothing could escape their scrutiny.

With a little exclamation he bent and picked up something from the floor.

It was a small square of cambric, very dainty. 'Our friend the *chef de train* was right. There is a woman concerned in this.'

'And most conveniently she leaves her handkerchief

85

behind!' said Poirot. 'Exactly as it happens in the books and on the films – and to make things even easier for us it is marked with an initial.'

'What a stroke of luck for us!' exclaimed the doctor.

'Is it not?' said Poirot.

Something in his tone surprised the doctor.

But before he could ask for elucidation, Poirot had made another dive on to the floor.

This time he held out on the palm of his hand – a pipe cleaner.

'It is perhaps the property of M. Ratchett?' suggested the doctor.

'There was no pipe in any of his pockets, and no tobacco or tobacco pouch.'

'Then it is a clue.'

'Oh! decidedly. And again dropped most conveniently. A masculine clue this time, you note! One cannot complain of having no clues in this case. There are clues here in abundance. By the way, what have you done with the weapon?'

'There was no sign of any weapon. The murderer must have taken it away with him.'

'I wonder why,' mused Poirot.

'Ah!' The doctor had been delicately exploring the pyjama pockets of the dead man.

'I overlooked this,' he said. 'I unbuttoned the jacket and threw it straight back.'

From the breast pocket he brought out a gold watch. The case was dented savagely, and the hands pointed to a quarter-past one.

'You see?' cried Constantine eagerly. 'This gives us the hour of the crime. It agrees with my calculations. Between midnight and two in the morning is what I said, and probably about one o'clock, though it is difficult to be exact in these matters. *Eh bien*, here is confirmation. A quarter-past one. That was the hour of the crime.'

'It is possible, yes. It is certainly possible.'

The doctor looked at him curiously.

'You will pardon me, M. Poirot, but I do not quite understand you.'

'I do not understand myself,' said Poirot. 'I understand nothing at all, and, as you perceive, it worries me.'

He sighed and bent over the little table, examining the charred fragment of paper. He murmured to himself.

'What I need at this moment is an old-fashioned woman's hat-box.'

Dr Constantine was at a loss to know what to make of this singular remark. In any case, Poirot gave him no time for questions. Opening the door into the corridor, he called for the conductor.

The man arrived at a run.

'How many women are there in this coach?'

The conductor counted on his fingers.

'One, two, three – six, Monsieur. The old American lady, a Swedish lady, the young English lady, the Countess Andrenyi and Madame la Princess Dragomiroff and her maid.'

Poirot considered.

'They all have hat-boxes, yes?'

'Yes, Monsieur.'

'Then bring me – let me see – yes, the Swedish lady's and that of the lady's-maid. Those two are the only hope. You will tell them it is a customs regulation – something – anything that occurs to you.'

'That will be all right Monsieur. Neither lady is in her compartment at the moment.'

'Then be quick.'

The conductor departed. He returned with the two hat-boxes. Poirot opened that of the lady's-maid and tossed it aside. Then he opened the Swedish lady's and uttered an exclamation of satisfaction. Removing the hats carefully, he disclosed round humps of wire-netting.

'Ah, here is what we need. About fifteen years ago hat-boxes were made like this. You skewered through the hat with a hatpin on to this hump of wire-netting.'

As he spoke he was skilfully removing two of

the attachments. Then he repacked the hat-box and told the conductor to return them both where they belonged.

When the door was shut once more he turned to his companion.

'See you, my dear doctor, me, I am not one to rely upon the expert procedure. It is the psychology I seek, not the fingerprint or the cigarette ash. But in this case I would welcome a little scientific assistance. This compartment is full of clues, but can I be sure that those clues are really what they seem to be?'

'I do not quite understand you, M. Poirot.'

'Well, to give you an example – we find a woman's handkerchief. Did a woman drop it? Or did a man, committing the crime, say to himself "I will make this look like a woman's crime. I will stab my enemy an unnecessary number of times, making some of the blows feeble and ineffective, and I will drop this handkerchief where no one can miss it." That is one possibility. Then there is another. Did a woman kill him and did she deliberately drop a pipe cleaner to make it look like a man's work? Or are we seriously to suppose that two people – a man and a woman – were separately concerned, and that each was so careless as to drop a clue to their identity? It is a little too much of a coincidence, that!'

'But where does the hat-box come in?' asked the doctor, still puzzled.

'Ah! I'm coming to that. As I say, these clues, the watch stopped at a quarter-past one, the handkerchief, the pipe cleaner, they may be genuine, or they may be fake. As to that I cannot yet tell. But there is *one* clue here which I believe – though again I may be wrong – has *not* been faked. I mean this flat match, M. le docteur. I *believe that that match was used by the murderer, not by M. Ratchett.* It was used to burn an incriminating paper of some kind. Possibly a note. If so, there was something in that note, some mistake, some error, that left a possible clue to the assailant. I am going to endeavour to resurrect what that something was.'

He went out of the compartment and returned a few moments later with a small spirit stove and a pair of curling tongs.

'I use them for the moustaches,' he said, referring to the latter.

The doctor watched him with great interest. He flattened out the two humps of wire, and with great care wriggled the charred scrap of paper on to one of them. He clapped the other on top of it and then, holding both pieces together with the tongs, held the whole thing over the flame of the spirit lamp.

'It is a very makeshift affair, this,' he said over

his shoulder. 'Let us hope that it will answer its purpose.'

The doctor watched the proceedings attentively. The metal began to glow. Suddenly he saw faint indications of letters. Words formed themselves slowly – words of fire.

It was a very tiny scrap. Only three words and a part of another showed.

'*—member little Daisy Armstrong.*'

'Ah!' Poirot gave a sharp exclamation.

'It tells you something?' asked the doctor.

Poirot's eyes were shining. He laid down the tongs carefully.

'Yes,' he said. '*I know the dead man's real name. I know why he had to leave America.*'

'What was his name?'

'Cassetti.'

'Cassetti.' Constantine knitted his brows. 'It brings back to me something. Some years ago. I cannot remember . . . It was a case in America, was it not?'

'Yes,' said Poirot. 'A case in America.'

Further than that Poirot was not disposed to be communicative. He looked round him as he went on:

'We will go into all that presently. Let us first make sure that we have seen all there is to be seen here.'

Agatha Christie

Quickly and deftly he went once more through the pockets of the dead man's clothes but found nothing there of interest. He tried the communicating door which led through to the next compartment, but it was bolted on the other side.

'There is one thing that I do not understand,' said Dr Constantine. 'If the murderer did not escape through the window, and if this communicating door was bolted on the other side, and if the door into the corridor was not only locked on the inside but chained, how then did the murderer leave the compartment?'

'That is what the audience says when a person bound hand and foot is shut into a cabinet – and disappears.'

'You mean –'

'I mean,' explained Poirot, 'that if the murderer intended us to believe that he had escaped by way of the window he would naturally make it appear that the other two exits were impossible. Like the "disappearing person" in the cabinet – it is a trick. It is our business to find out how the trick is done.'

He locked the communicating door on their side.

'In case,' he said, 'the excellent Mrs Hubbard should take it into her head to acquire first-hand details of the crime to write to her daughter.'

He looked round once more.

'There is nothing more to do here, I think. Let us rejoin M. Bouc.'

Chapter 8

The Armstrong Kidnapping Case

They found M. Bouc finishing an omelet.

'I thought it best to have lunch served immediately in the restaurant-car,' he said. 'Afterwards it will be cleared and M. Poirot can conduct his examination of the passengers there. In the meantime I have ordered them to bring us three some food here.'

'An excellent idea,' said Poirot.

Neither of the other two men was hungry, and the meal was soon eaten, but not till they were sipping their coffee did M. Bouc mention the subject that was occupying all their minds.

'*Eh bien?*' he asked.

'*Eh bien*, I have discovered the identity of the victim. I know why it was imperative he should leave America.'

'Who was he?'

'Do you remember reading of the Armstrong baby?

Agatha Christie

This is the man who murdered little Daisy Armstrong – Cassetti.'

'I recall it now. A shocking affair – though I cannot remember the details.'

'Colonel Armstrong was an Englishman – a V.C. He was half American, as his mother was a daughter of W.K. Van der Halt, the Wall Street millionaire. He married the daughter of Linda Arden, the most famous tragic American actress of her day. They lived in America and had one child – a girl – whom they idolized. When she was three years old she was kidnapped, and an impossibly high sum demanded as the price of her return. I will not weary you with all the intricacies that followed. I will come to the moment, when, after having paid over the enormous sum of two hundred thousand dollars, the child's dead body was discovered, it having been dead at least a fortnight. Public indignation rose to fever point. And there was worse to follow. Mrs Armstrong was expecting another child. Following the shock of the discovery, she gave birth to a dead child born prematurely, and herself died. Her broken-hearted husband shot himself.'

'*Mon Dieu*, what a tragedy. I remember now,' said M. Bouc. 'There was also another death, if I remember rightly?'

'Yes – an unfortunate French or Swiss nursemaid.

The police were convinced that she had some knowledge of the crime. They refused to believe her hysterical denials. Finally, in a fit of despair, the poor girl threw herself from a window and was killed. It was proved afterwards that she was absolutely innocent of any complicity in the crime.'

'It is not good to think of,' said M. Bouc.

'About six months later, this man Cassetti was arrested as the head of the gang who had kidnapped the child. They had used the same methods in the past. If the police seemed likely to get on their trail, they had killed their prisoner, hidden the body, and continued to extract as much money as possible before the crime was discovered.

'Now, I will make clear to you this, my friend. Cassetti was the man! But by means of the enormous wealth he had piled up and by the secret hold he had over various persons, he was acquitted on some technical inaccuracy. Notwithstanding that, he would have been lynched by the populace had he not been clever enough to give them the slip. It is now clear to me what happened. He changed his name and left America. Since then he has been a gentleman of leisure, travelling abroad and living on his *rentes*.'

'*Ah! quel animal!*' M. Bouc's tone was redolent of heartfelt disgust. 'I cannot regret that he is dead – not at all!'

'I agree with you.'

'*Tout de même*, it is not necessary that he should be killed on the Orient Express. There are other places.'

Poirot smiled a little. He realized that M. Bouc was biased in the matter.

'The question we have now to ask ourselves is this,' he said. 'Is this murder the work of some rival gang whom Cassetti had double-crossed in the past, or is it an act of private vengeance?'

He explained his discovery of the few words on the charred fragment of paper.

'If I am right in my assumption, then the letter was burnt by the murderer. Why? Because it mentioned the word "Armstrong," which is the clue to the mystery.'

'Are there any members of the Armstrong family living?'

'That, unfortunately, I do not know. I think I remember reading of a younger sister of Mrs Armstrong's.'

Poirot went on to relate the joint conclusions of himself and Dr Constantine. M. Bouc brightened at the mention of the broken watch.

'That seems to give us the time of the crime very exactly.'

'Yes,' said Poirot. 'It is very convenient.'

There was an indescribable something in his tone that made both the other two look at him curiously.

'You say that you yourself heard Ratchett speak to the conductor at twenty minutes to one?'

Poirot related just what had occurred.

'Well,' said M. Bouc, 'that proves at least that Cassetti – or Ratchett, as I shall continue to call him – was certainly alive at twenty minutes to one.'

'Twenty-three minutes to one, to be precise.'

'Then at twelve thirty-seven, to put it formally, M. Ratchett was alive. That is *one* fact, at least.'

Poirot did not reply. He sat looking thoughtfully in front of him.

There was a tap on the door, and the restaurant attendant entered.

'The restaurant-car is free now, Monsieur,' he said.

'We will go there,' said M. Bouc, rising.

'I may accompany you?' asked Constantine.

'Certainly, my dear doctor. Unless M. Poirot has any objection?'

'Not at all. Not at all,' said Poirot.

After a little politeness in the matter of procedure, '*Après vous, Monsieur.*' '*Mais non, après vous,*' they left the compartment.

Part 2

The Evidence

Chapter 1

The Evidence of the Wagon Lit Conductor

In the restaurant-car all was in readiness.

Poirot and M. Bouc sat together on one side of a table. The doctor sat across the aisle.

On the table in front of Poirot was a plan of the Istanbul-Calais coach with the names of the passengers marked in in red ink.

The passports and tickets were in a pile at one side. There was writing paper, ink, pen and pencils.

'Excellent,' said Poirot. 'We can open our Court of Inquiry without more ado. First, I think, we should take the evidence of the Wagon Lit conductor. You probably know something about the man. What character has he? Is he a man in whose word you would place reliance?'

'I should say so most assuredly. Pierre Michel has been employed by the company for over fifteen years.

He is a Frenchman – lives near Calais. Thoroughly respectable and honest. Not, perhaps, remarkable for brains.'

Poirot nodded comprehendingly.

'Good,' he said. 'Let us see him.'

Pierre Michel had recovered some of his assurance, but he was still extremely nervous.

'I hope Monsieur will not think that there has been any negligence on my part,' he said anxiously, his eyes going from Poirot to M. Bouc. 'It is a terrible thing that has happened. I hope Monsieur does not think that it reflects on me in any way?'

Having soothed the man's fears, Poirot began his questions. He first elicited Michel's name and address, his length of service, and the length of time he had been on this particular route. These particulars he already knew, but the routine questions served to put the man at his ease.

'And now,' went on Poirot, 'let us come to the events of last night. M. Ratchett retired to bed – when?'

'Almost immediately after dinner, Monsieur. Actually before we left Belgrade. So he did on the previous night. He had directed me to make up the bed while he was at dinner, and I did so.'

'Did anybody go into his compartment afterwards?'

'His valet, Monsieur, and the young American gentleman his secretary.'

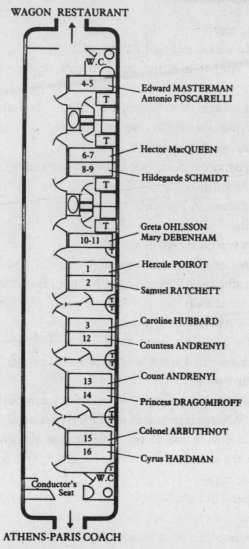

WAGON RESTAURANT

W.C.

4-5 — Edward MASTERMAN
Antonio FOSCARELLI

T

T

6-7 — Hector MacQUEEN

8-9 — Hildegarde SCHMIDT

T

T

Greta OHLSSON
10-11 — Mary DEBENHAM

T

1 — Hercule POIROT

2 — Samuel RATCHETT

T

3 — Caroline HUBBARD

12 — Countess ANDRENYI

T
T

13 — Count ANDRENYI

14 — Princess DRAGOMIROFF

T
T

15 — Colonel ARBUTHNOT

16 — Cyrus HARDMAN

T

W.C

Conductor's
Seat

ATHENS-PARIS COACH

'Anyone else?'

'No, Monsieur, not that I know of.'

'Good. And that is the last you saw or heard of him?'

'No, Monsieur. You forget, he rang his bell about twenty to one – soon after we had stopped.'

'What happened exactly?'

'I knocked at the door, but he called out and said he had made a mistake.'

'In English or in French?'

'In French.'

'What were his words exactly?'

'*Ce n'est rien. Je me suis trompé.*'

'Quite right,' said Poirot. 'That is what I heard. And then you went away?'

'Yes, Monsieur.'

'Did you go back to your seat?'

'No, Monsieur, I went first to answer another bell that had just rung.'

'Now, Michel, I am going to ask you an important question. Where were you at a quarter-past one?'

'I, Monsieur? I was at my little seat at the end – facing up the corridor.'

'You are sure?'

'*Mais oui* – at least –'

'Yes?'

'I went into the next coach, the Athens coach, to

speak to my colleague there. We spoke about the snow. That was at some time soon after one o'clock. I cannot say exactly.'

'And you returned – when?'

'One of my bells rang, Monsieur – I remember – I told you. It was the American lady. She had rung several times.'

'I recollect,' said Poirot. 'And after that?'

'After that, Monsieur? I answered your bell and brought you some mineral water. Then, about half an hour later, I made up the bed in one of the other compartments – that of the young American gentle-man, M. Ratchett's secretary.'

'Was M. MacQueen alone in his compartment when you went to make up his bed?'

'The English Colonel from No. 15 was with him. They had been sitting talking.'

'What did the Colonel do when he left M. MacQueen?'

'He went back to his own compartment.'

'No. 15 – that is quite close to your seat, is it not?'

'Yes, Monsieur, it is the second compartment from that end of the corridor.'

'His bed was already made up?'

'Yes, Monsieur. I had made it up while he was at dinner.'

'What time was all this?'

'I could not say exactly, Monsieur. Not later than two o'clock, certainly.'

'And after that?'

'After that, Monsieur, I sat in my seat till morning.'

'You did not go again into the Athens coach?'

'No, Monsieur.'

'Perhaps you slept?'

'I do not think so, Monsieur. The train being at a standstill prevented me from dozing off as I usually do.'

'Did you see any of the passengers moving up or down the corridor?'

The man reflected.

'One of the ladies went to the toilet at the far end, I think.'

'Which lady?'

'I do not know, Monsieur. It was far down the corridor, and she had her back to me. She had on a kimono of scarlet with dragons on it.'

Poirot nodded.

'And after that?'

'Nothing, Monsieur, until the morning.'

'You are sure?'

'Ah, pardon, you yourself, Monsieur, opened your door and looked out for a second.'

'Good, my friend,' said Poirot. 'I wondered whether you would remember that. By the way, I was awakened by what sounded like something heavy falling against my door. Have you any idea what that could have been?'

The man stared at him.

'There was nothing, Monsieur. Nothing, I am positive of it.'

'Then I must have had the *cauchemar*,' said Poirot philosophically.

'Unless,' said M. Bouc, 'it was something in the compartment next door that you heard.'

Poirot took no notice of the suggestion. Perhaps he did not wish to before the Wagon Lit conductor.

'Let us pass to another point,' he said. 'Supposing that last night an assassin joined the train. It is quite certain that he could not have left it after committing the crime?'

Pierre Michel shook his head.

'Nor that he can be concealed on it somewhere?'

'It has been well searched,' said M. Bouc. 'Abandon that idea, my friend.'

'Besides,' said Michel, 'no one could get on to the sleeping-car without my seeing them.'

'When was the last stop?'

'Vincovci.'

'What time was that?'

'We should have left there at 11.58. But owing to the weather we were twenty minutes late.'

'Someone might have come along from the ordinary part of the train?'

'No, Monsieur. After the service of dinner the door between the ordinary carriages and the sleeping-cars is locked.'

'Did you yourself descend from the train at Vincovci?'

'Yes, Monsieur. I got down on to the platform as usual and stood by the step up into the train. The other conductors did the same.'

'What about the forward door? The one near the restaurant-car?'

'It is always fastened on the inside.'

'It is not so fastened now.'

The man looked surprised, then his face cleared.

'Doubtless one of the passengers has opened it to look out on the snow.'

'Probably,' said Poirot.

He tapped thoughtfully on the table for a minute or two.

'Monsieur does not blame me?' said the man timidly.

Poirot smiled on him kindly.

'You have had the evil chance, my friend,' he said. 'Ah! One other point while I remember it. You said that another bell rang just as you were knocking at M. Ratchett's door. In fact, I heard it myself. Whose was it?'

'It was the bell of Madame la Princesse Dragomiroff. She desired me to summon her maid.'

'And you did so?'

'Yes, Monsieur.'

Poirot studied the plan in front of him thoughtfully. Then he inclined his head.

'That is all,' he said, 'for the moment.'

'Thank you, Monsieur.'

The man rose. He looked at M. Bouc.

'Do not distress yourself,' said the latter kindly. 'I cannot see that there has been any negligence on your part.'

Gratified, Pierre Michel left the compartment.

Chapter 2

The Evidence of the Secretary

For a minute or two Poirot remained lost in thought.

'I think,' he said at last, 'that it would be well to have a further word with M. MacQueen, in view of what we now know.'

The young American appeared promptly.

'Well,' he said, 'how are things going?'

'Not too badly. Since our last conversation I have learnt something – the identity of M. Ratchett.'

Hector MacQueen leaned forward interestedly.

'Yes?' he said.

'Ratchett, as you suspected, was merely an alias. Ratchett was Cassetti, the man who ran the celebrated kidnapping stunts – including the famous affair of little Daisy Armstrong.'

An expression of utter astonishment appeared on MacQueen's face; then it darkened.

'The damned skunk!' he exclaimed.

'You had no idea of this, M. MacQueen?'

'No, sir,' said the young American decidedly. 'If I had I'd have cut off my right hand before it had a chance to do secretarial work for him!'

'You feel strongly about the matter, M. MacQueen?'

'I have a particular reason for doing so. My father was the district attorney who handled the case, M. Poirot. I saw Mrs Armstrong more than once – she was a lovely woman. So gentle and heartbroken.' His face darkened. 'If ever a man deserved what he got, Ratchett or Cassetti is the man. I'm rejoiced at his end. Such a man wasn't fit to live!'

'You almost feel as though you would have been willing to do the good deed yourself?'

'I do. I –' He paused, then flushed rather guiltily. 'Seems I'm kind of incriminating myself.'

'I should be more inclined to suspect you, M. MacQueen, if you displayed an inordinate sorrow at your employer's decease.'

'I don't think I could do that, even to save myself from the chair,' said MacQueen grimly.

Then he added:

'If I'm not being unduly curious, just how did you figure this out? Cassetti's identity, I mean.'

'By a fragment of a letter found in his compartment.'

'But surely – I mean – that was rather careless of the old man?'

'That depends,' said Poirot, 'on the point of view.'

The young man seemed to find this remark rather baffling. He stared at Poirot as though trying to make him out.

'The task before me,' said Poirot, 'is to make sure of the movements of everyone on the train. No offence need be taken, you understand? It is only a matter of routine.'

'Sure. Get right on with it and let me clear my character if I can.'

'I need hardly ask you the number of your compartment,' said Poirot, smiling, 'since I shared it with you for a night. It is the second-class compartment Nos. 6 and 7, and after my departure you had it to yourself.'

'That's right.'

'Now, M. MacQueen, I want you to describe your movements last night from the time of leaving the dining-car.'

'That's quite easy. I went back to my compartment, read a bit, got out on the platform at Belgrade, decided it was too cold, and got in again. I talked for a while to a young English lady who is in the compartment next to mine. Then I fell into conversation with that Englishman, Colonel Arbuthnot – as a matter of fact I think you passed us as we were talking. Then I went in to Mr Ratchett and, as I told you, took down some memoranda of letters he wanted written. I said good-night to him and left him. Colonel Arbuthnot was still standing in the corridor. His compartment was already made up for the night, so I suggested that he should come along to mine. I ordered a couple of drinks and we got right down to it. Discussed world politics and the Government of India and our own troubles with the financial situation and the Wall Street crisis. I don't as a rule cotton to Britishers – they're a stiff-necked lot – but I liked this one.'

'Do you know what time it was when he left you?'

'Pretty late. Getting on for two o'clock, I should say.'

'You noticed that the train had stopped?'

'Oh, yes. We wondered a bit. Looked out and saw the snow lying very thick, but we didn't think it was serious.'

'What happened when Colonel Arbuthnot finally said good-night?'

'He went along to his compartment and I called to the conductor to make up my bed.'

'Where were you whilst he was making it?'

'Standing just outside the door in the corridor smoking a cigarette.'

'And then?'

'And then I went to bed and slept till morning.'

'During the evening did you leave the train at all?'

'Arbuthnot and I thought we'd get out at – what was

the name of the place? – Vincovci to stretch our legs a bit. But it was bitterly cold – a blizzard on. We soon hopped back again.'

'By which door did you leave the train?'

'By the one nearest to our compartment.'

'The one next to the dining-car?'

'Yes.'

'Do you remember if it was bolted?'

MacQueen considered.

'Why, yes, I seem to remember it was. At least there was a kind of bar that fitted across the handle. Is that what you mean?'

'Yes. On getting back into the train did you replace that bar?'

'Why, no – I don't think I did. I got in last. No, I don't seem to remember doing so.'

He added suddenly:

'Is that an important point?'

'It may be. Now, I presume, Monsieur, that while you and Colonel Arbuthnot were sitting talking the door of your compartment into the corridor was open?'

Hector MacQueen nodded.

'I want you, if you can, to tell me if anyone passed along that corridor *after* the train left Vincovci until the time you parted company for the night.'

MacQueen drew his brows together.

'I think the conductor passed along once,' he said,

'coming from the direction of the dining-car. And a woman passed the other way, going towards it.'

'Which woman?'

'I couldn't say. I didn't really notice. You see, I was just arguing a point with Arbuthnot. I just seem to remember a glimpse of some scarlet silk affair passing the door. I didn't look, and anyway I wouldn't have seen the person's face. As you know, my carriage faces the dining-car end of the train, so a woman going along the corridor in that direction would have her back to me as soon as she passed.'

Poirot nodded.

'She was going to the toilet, I presume?'

'I suppose so.'

'And you saw her return?'

'Well, no, now that you mention it, I didn't notice her returning, but I suppose she must have done so.'

'One more question. Do you smoke a pipe, M. MacQueen?'

'No, sir, I do not.'

Poirot paused a moment.

'I think that is all at present. I should now like to see the valet of M. Ratchett. By the way, did both you and he always travel second-class?'

'He did. But I usually went first – if possible in the adjoining compartment to Mr Ratchett. Then he had most of his baggage put in my compartment and yet could get at both it and me easily whenever he chose. But on this occasion all the first-class berths were booked except the one which he took.'

'I comprehend. Thank you, M. MacQueen.'

Chapter 3

The Evidence of the Valet

The American was succeeded by the pale Englishman with the inexpressive face whom Poirot had already noticed on the day before. He stood waiting very correctly. Poirot motioned to him to sit down.

'You are, I understand, the valet of M. Ratchett?'

'Yes, sir.'

'Your name?'

'Edward Henry Masterman.'

'Your age?'

'Thirty-nine.'

'And your home address?'

'21 Friar Street, Clerkenwell.'

'You have heard that your master has been murdered?'

'Yes, sir. A very shocking occurrence.'

'Will you now tell me, please, at what hour you last saw M. Ratchett?'

The valet considered.

'It must have been about nine o'clock, sir, last night. That or a little after.'

'Tell me in your own words exactly what happened.'

'I went in to Mr Ratchett as usual, sir, and attended to his wants.'

'What were your duties exactly?'

'To fold or hang up his clothes, sir. Put his dental plate in water and see that he had everything he wanted for the night.'

'Was his manner much the same as usual?'

The valet considered a moment.

'Well, sir, I think he was upset.'

'In what way – upset?'

'Over a letter he'd been reading. He asked me if it was I who had put it in his compartment. Of course I told him I hadn't done any such thing, but he swore at me and found fault with everything I did.'

'Was that unusual?'

'Oh, no, sir, he lost his temper easily – as I say, it just depended what had happened to upset him.'

'Did your master ever take a sleeping draught?'

Dr Constantine leaned forward a little.

'Always when travelling by train, sir. He said he couldn't sleep otherwise.'

'Do you know what drug he was in the habit of taking?'

'I couldn't say, I'm sure, sir. There was no name on the bottle. Just "*The Sleeping Draught to be taken at bedtime.*"'

'Did he take it last night?'

'Yes, sir. I poured it into a glass and put it on top of the toilet table ready for him.'

'You didn't actually see him drink it?'

'No, sir.'

'What happened next?'

'I asked if there was anything further, and asked what time M. Ratchett would like to be called in the morning. He said he didn't want to be disturbed till he rang.'

'Was that usual?'

'Quite usual, sir. He used to ring the bell for the conductor and then send him for me when he was ready to get up.'

'Was he usually an early or a late riser?'

'It depended, sir, on his mood. Sometimes he'd get up for breakfast, sometimes he wouldn't get up till just on lunch time.'

'So that you weren't alarmed when the morning wore on and no summons came?'

'No, sir.'

'Did you know that your master had enemies?'

'Yes, sir.'

The man spoke quite unemotionally.

'How did you know?'

'I had heard him discussing some letters, sir, with Mr MacQueen.'

'Had you an affection for your employer, Masterman?'

Masterman's face became, if possible, even more inexpressive than it was normally.

'I should hardly like to say that, sir. He was a generous employer.'

'But you didn't like him?'

'Shall we put it that I don't care very much for Americans, sir.'

'Have you ever been in America?'

'No, sir.'

'Do you remember reading in the paper of the Armstrong kidnapping case?'

A little colour came into the man's cheeks.

'Yes, indeed, sir. A little baby girl, wasn't it? A very shocking affair.'

'Did you know that your employer, M. Ratchett, was the principal instigator in that affair?'

'No, indeed, sir.' The valet's tone held positive warmth and feeling for the first time. 'I can hardly believe it, sir.'

'Nevertheless, it is true. Now, to pass to your own movements last night. A matter of routine, you understand. What did you do after leaving your master?'

'I told Mr MacQueen, sir, that the master wanted him. Then I went to my own compartment and read.'

'Your compartment was −?'

'The end second-class one, sir. Next to the dining-car.'

Poirot was looking at his plan.

'I see − and you had which berth?'

'The lower one, sir.'

'That is No. 4?'

'Yes, sir.'

'Is there anyone in with you?'

'Yes, sir. A big Italian fellow.'

'Does he speak English?'

'Well, a kind of English, sir.' The valet's tone was deprecating. 'He's been in America − Chicago − I understand.'

'Do you and he talk together much?'

'No, sir. I prefer to read.'

Poirot smiled. He could visualize the scene − the large voluble Italian, and the snub direct administered by the gentleman's gentleman.

'And what, may I ask, are you reading?' he inquired.

'At present, sir, I am reading *Love's Captive*, by Mrs Arabella Richardson.'

'A good story?'

'I find it highly enjoyable, sir.'

'Well, let us continue. You returned to your compartment and read *Love's Captive* till − when?'

'At about ten-thirty, sir, this Italian wanted to go

to bed. So the conductor came and made the beds up.'

'And then you went to bed and to sleep?'

'I went to bed, sir, but I didn't sleep.'

'Why didn't you sleep?'

'I had the toothache, sir.'

'Oh, *là là* – that is painful.'

'Most painful, sir.'

'Did you do anything for it?'

'I applied a little oil of cloves, sir, which relieved the pain a little, but I was still not able to get to sleep. I turned the light on above my head and continued to read – to take my mind off it, as it were.'

'And did you not go to sleep at all?'

'Yes, sir, I dropped off about four in the morning.'

'And your companion?'

'The Italian fellow? Oh, he just snored.'

'He did not leave the compartment at all during the night?'

'No, sir.'

'Did you?'

'No, sir.'

'Did you hear anything during the night?'

'I don't think so, sir. Nothing unusual, I mean. The train being at a standstill made it all very quiet.'

Poirot was silent a moment or two, then he said:

'Well, I think there is very little more to be said. You cannot throw any light upon the tragedy?'

'I'm afraid not. I'm sorry, sir.'

'As far as you know, was there any quarrel or bad blood between your master and M. MacQueen?'

'Oh, no, sir. Mr MacQueen was a very pleasant gentleman.'

'Where were you in service before you came to M. Ratchett?'

'With Sir Henry Tomlinson, sir, in Grosvenor Square.'

'Why did you leave him?'

'He was going to East Africa, sir, and did not require my services any longer. But I am sure he will speak for me, sir. I was with him some years.'

'And you have been with M. Ratchett – how long?'

'Just over nine months, sir.'

'Thank you, Masterman. By the way, are you a pipe smoker?'

'No, sir. I only smoke cigarettes – gaspers, sir.'

'Thank you. That will do.'

The valet hesitated a moment.

'You'll excuse me, sir, but the elderly American lady is in what I might describe as a state, sir. She's saying she knows all about the murderer. She's in a very excitable condition, sir.'

'In that case,' said Poirot, smiling, 'we had better see her next.'

'Shall I tell her, sir? She's been demanding to see someone in authority for a long time. The conductor's been trying to pacify her.'

'Send her to us, my friend,' said Poirot. 'We will listen to her story now.'

Chapter 4

The Evidence of the American Lady

Mrs Hubbard arrived in the dining-car in such a state of breathless excitement that she was hardly able to articulate her words.

'Now just tell me this. Who's in authority here? I've got some *vurry* important information, *vurry* important, indeed, and I just want to tell it to someone in authority as soon as may be. If you gentlemen –'

Her wavering glance fluctuated between the three men. Poirot leaned forward.

'Tell it to me, Madame,' he said. 'But, first, pray be seated.'

Mrs Hubbard plumped heavily down on to the seat opposite to him.

'What I've got to tell you is just this. There was a murder on the train last night, and the murderer was *right there in my compartment!*'

She paused to give dramatic emphasis to her words.

'You are sure of this, Madame?'

'Of course I'm sure! The idea! I know what I'm talking about. I'll tell you just everything there is to tell. I'd gotten into bed and gone to sleep, and suddenly I woke up – all in the dark, it was – and I knew there was a man in my compartment. I was just so scared I couldn't scream, if you know what I mean. I just lay there and thought, "Mercy, I'm going to be killed." I just can't describe to you how I felt. These nasty trains, I thought, and all the outrages I'd read of. And I thought, "Well, anyway, he won't get my jewellery." Because, you see, I'd put that in a stocking and hidden it under my pillow – which isn't so mighty comfortable, by the way, kinder bumpy, if you know what I mean. But that's neither here nor there. Where was I?'

'You realized, Madame, that there was a man in your compartment.'

'Yes, well, I just lay there with my eyes closed, and I thought whatever should I do, and I thought, "Well, I'm just thankful that my daughter doesn't know the plight I'm in." And then, somehow, I got my wits about me and I felt about with my hand and I pressed the bell for the conductor. I pressed it and I pressed it, but nothing happened, and I can tell you I thought my heart was going to stop beating. "Mercy," I said to myself, "maybe they've murdered every single soul on the train." It was at a standstill, anyhow, and a nasty quiet feel in the air. But I just went on pressing that bell, and oh! the relief when I heard footsteps coming running down the corridor and a knock on the door. "Come in," I screamed, and I switched on the lights at the same time. And, would you believe it, there wasn't a soul there.'

This seemed to Mrs Hubbard to be a dramatic climax rather than an anti-climax.

'And what happened next, Madame?'

'Why, I told the man what had happened, and he didn't seem to believe me. Seemed to imagine I'd dreamt the whole thing. I made him look under the seat, though he said there wasn't room for a man to squeeze himself in there. It was plain enough the man had got away, but there *had* been a man there and it just made me mad the way the conductor tried to soothe me down! I'm not one to imagine things, Mr – I don't think I know your name?'

'Poirot, Madame, and this is M. Bouc, a director of the company, and Dr Constantine.'

Mrs Hubbard murmured:

'Pleased to meet you, I'm sure,' to all three of them in an abstracted manner, and then plunged once more into her recital.

'Now I'm just not going to pretend I was as bright as I might have been. I got it into my head that it was the man from next door – the poor fellow who's been killed. I told the conductor to look at the door between the compartments, and sure enough it wasn't bolted. Well, I soon saw to that, I told him to bolt it then and there, and after he'd gone out I got up and put a suitcase against it to make sure.'

'What time was this, Mrs Hubbard?'

'Well, I'm sure I can't tell you. I never looked to see. I was so upset.'

'And what is your theory now?'

'Why, I should say it was just as plain as plain could be. The man in my compartment was the murderer. Who else could he be?'

'And you think he went back into the adjoining compartment?'

'How do I know where he went? I had my eyes tight shut.'

'He must have slipped out through the door into the corridor.'

'Well, I couldn't say. You see, I had my eyes tight shut.'

Mrs Hubbard sighed convulsively.

'Mercy, I was scared! If my daughter only knew –'

'You do not think, Madame, that what you heard was the noise of someone moving about next door – in the murdered man's compartment?'

'No, I do not, Mr – what is it? – Poirot. The man

was *right there in the same compartment with me.* And, what's more, I've got proof of it.'

Triumphantly she hauled a large handbag into view and proceeded to burrow in its interior.

She took out in turn two large clean handkerchiefs, a pair of horn-rimmed glasses, a bottle of aspirin, a packet of Glauber's salts, a celluloid tube of bright green peppermints, a bunch of keys, a pair of scissors, a book of American Express cheques, a snapshot of an extraordinarily plain-looking child, some letters, five strings of pseudo Oriental beads and a small metal object – a button.

'You see this button? Well, it's not one of *my* buttons. It's not off anything I've got. I found it this morning when I got up.'

As she placed it on the table, M. Bouc leaned forward and gave an exclamation.

'But this is a button from the tunic of a Wagon Lit attendant!'

'There may be a natural explanation for that,' said Poirot.

He turned gently to the lady.

'This button, Madame, may have dropped from the conductor's uniform, either when he searched your cabin, or when he was making the bed up last night.'

'I just don't know what's the matter with all you people. Seems as though you don't do anything but make objections. Now listen here. I was reading a magazine last night before I went to sleep. Before I turned the light out I placed that magazine on a little case that was standing on the floor near the window. Have you got that?'

They assured her that they had.

'Very well, then. The conductor looked under the seat from near the door and then he came in and bolted the door between me and the next compartment, but he never went up near the window. Well, this morning that button was lying right on top of the magazine. What do you call that, I should like to know?'

'That, Madame, I call evidence,' said Poirot.

The answer seemed to appease the lady.

'It makes me madder than a hornet to be disbelieved,' she explained.

'You have given us most interesting and valuable evidence,' said Poirot soothingly. 'Now, may I ask you a few questions?'

'Why, willingly.'

'How was it, since you were nervous of this man Ratchett, that you hadn't already bolted the door between the compartments?'

'I had,' returned Mrs Hubbard promptly.

'Oh, you had?'

'Well, as a matter of fact, I asked that Swedish

creature – a pleasant soul – if it was bolted, and she said it was.'

'How was it you couldn't see for yourself?'

'Because I was in bed and my sponge-bag was hanging on the door handle.'

'What time was it when you asked her to do this for you?'

'Now let me think. It must have been round about half-past ten or a quarter to eleven. She'd come along to see if I'd got an aspirin. I told her where to find it, and she got it out of my grip.'

'You yourself were in bed?'

'Yes.'

Suddenly she laughed.

'Poor soul – she was in quite a taking. You see, she'd opened the door of the next compartment by mistake.'

'M. Ratchett's?'

'Yes. You know how difficult it is as you come along the train and all the doors are shut. She opened his by mistake. She was very distressed about it. He'd laughed, it seemed, and I fancy he may have said something not quite nice. Poor thing, she was all in a flutter. "Oh! I make mistake," she said. "I ashamed make mistake. Not nice man," she said. "He say, 'You too old.'"'

Dr Constantine sniggered and Mrs Hubbard immediately froze him with a glance.

'He wasn't a nice kind of man,' she said, 'to say a thing like that to a lady. It's not right to laugh at such things.'

Dr Constantine hastily apologized.

'Did you hear any noise from M. Ratchett's compartment after that?' asked Poirot.

'Well – not exactly.'

'What do you mean by that, Madame?'

'Well –' she paused. 'He snored.'

'Ah! he snored, did he?'

'Terribly. The night before it quite kept me awake.'

'You didn't hear him snore after you had had the scare about a man being in your compartment?'

'Why, Mr Poirot, how could I? He was dead.'

'Ah, yes, truly,' said Poirot. He appeared confused.

'Do you remember the affair of the Armstrong kidnapping, Mrs Hubbard?' he asked.

'Yes, indeed I do. And how the wretch that did it escaped scot free! My, I'd have liked to get my hands on him.'

'He has not escaped. He is dead. He died last night.'

'You don't mean –?' Mrs Hubbard half rose from her chair in excitement.

'But yes, I do. Ratchett was the man.'

'*Well*! Well, to think of that! I must write and tell my daughter. Now, didn't I tell you last night that that man had an evil face? I was right, you see. My daughter always says: "When Momma's got a hunch, you can bet your bottom dollar it's O.K."'

'Were you acquainted with any of the Armstrong family, Mrs Hubbard?'

'No. They moved in a very exclusive circle. But I've always heard that Mrs Armstrong was a perfectly lovely woman and that her husband worshipped her.'

'Well, Mrs Hubbard, you have helped us very much – very much indeed. Perhaps you will give me your full name?'

'Why, certainly. Caroline Martha Hubbard.'

'Will you write your address down here?'

Mrs Hubbard did so, without ceasing to speak.

'I just can't get over it. Cassetti – on this train. I had a hunch about that man, didn't I, Mr Poirot?'

'Yes, indeed, Madame. By the way, have you a scarlet silk dressing-gown?'

'Mercy, what an odd question! Why, no. I've got two dressing-gowns with me – a pink flannel one that's kind of cosy for on board ship, and one my daughter gave me as a present – a kind of local affair in purple silk. But what in creation do you want to know about my dressing-gowns for?'

'Well, you see, Madame, someone in a scarlet kimono entered either your or Mr Ratchett's compartment last night. It is, as you said just now, very difficult when all the doors are shut to know which compartment is which.'

'Well, no one in a scarlet dressing-gown came into my compartment.'

'Then she must have gone into M. Ratchett's.'

Mrs Hubbard pursed her lips together and said grimly:

'That wouldn't surprise me any.'

Poirot leaned forward.

'So you heard a woman's voice next door?'

'I don't know how you guessed that, Mr Poirot. I don't really. But – well – as a matter of fact, I *did*.'

'But when I asked you just now if you heard anything next door, you only said you heard Mr Ratchett snoring.'

'Well that was true enough. He *did* snore part of the time. As for the other –' Mrs Hubbard got rather pink. 'It isn't a very nice thing to speak about.'

'What time was it when you heard a woman's voice?'

'I can't tell you. I just woke up for a minute and heard a woman talking, and it was plain enough where she was. So I just thought, "Well that's the kind of man he is. Well, I'm not surprised," and then I went to sleep again, and I'm sure I should never have mentioned anything of the kind to three strange gentlemen if you hadn't dragged it out of me.'

'Was it before the scare about the man in your compartment, or after?'

'Why, that's like what you said just now! He wouldn't have had a woman talking to him if he were dead, would he?'

'*Pardon*. You must think me very stupid, Madame.'

'I guess even you get kinder muddled now and then. I just can't get over it being that monster Cassetti. What my daughter will say –'

Poirot managed adroitly to help the good lady to restore the contents of her handbag and he then shepherded her towards the door.

At the last moment he said:

'You have dropped your handkerchief, Madame.'

Mrs Hubbard looked at the little scrap of cambric he held out to her.

'That's not mine, Mr Poirot. I've got mine right here.'

'*Pardon*. I thought as it had the initial H on it –'

'Well, now, that's curious, but it's certainly not mine. Mine are marked C.M.H., and they're sensible things – not expensive Paris fallals. What good is a handkerchief like that to anybody's nose?'

Neither of the three men seemed to have an answer to this question, and Mrs Hubbard sailed out triumphantly.

Chapter 5

The Evidence of the Swedish Lady

M. Bouc was handling the button Mrs Hubbard had left behind her.

'This button. I cannot understand it. Does it mean that, after all, Pierre Michel is involved in some way?' he said. He paused, then continued, as Poirot did not reply. 'What have you to say, my friend?'

'That button, it suggests possibilities,' said Poirot thoughtfully. 'Let us interview next the Swedish lady before we discuss the evidence we have heard.'

He sorted through the pile of passports in front of him.

'Ah! here we are. Greta Ohlsson, age forty-nine.'

M. Bouc gave directions to the restaurant attendant, and presently the lady with the yellowish-grey bun of hair and the long mild sheep-like face was ushered in. She peered short-sightedly at Poirot through her glasses, but was quite calm.

It transpired that she understood and spoke French, so that the conversation took place in that language. Poirot first asked her the questions to which he already knew the answers – her name, age, and address. He then asked her her occupation.

She was, she told him, matron in a missionary school near Stamboul. She was a trained nurse.

'You know, of course, of what took place last night, Mademoiselle?'

'Naturally. It is very dreadful. And the American lady tells me that the murderer was actually in her compartment.'

'I hear, Mademoiselle, that you were the last person to see the murdered man alive?'

'I do not know. It may be so. I opened the door of his compartment by mistake. I was much ashamed. It was a most awkward mistake.'

'You actually saw him?'

'Yes. He was reading a book. I apologized quickly and withdrew.'

'Did he say anything to you?'

A slight flush showed on the worthy lady's cheek.

'He laughed and said a few words. I – I did not quite catch them.'

'And what did you do after that, Mademoiselle?' asked Poirot, passing from the subject tactfully.

'I went in to the American lady, Mrs Hubbard. I

asked her for some aspirin and she gave it to me.'

'Did she ask you whether the communicating door between her compartment and that of M. Ratchett was bolted?'

'Yes.'

'And was it?'

'Yes.'

'And after that?'

'After that I go back to my own compartment, I take the aspirin and lie down.'

'What time was all this?'

'When I got into bed it was five minutes to eleven, because I look at my watch before I wind it up.'

'Did you go to sleep quickly?'

'Not very quickly. My head got better, but I lay awake some time.'

'Had the train come to a stop before you went to sleep?'

'I do not think so. We stopped, I think, at a station, just as I was getting drowsy.'

'That would be Vincovci. Now your compartment, Mademoiselle, is this one?' he indicated it on the plan.

'That is so, yes.'

'You had the upper or the lower berth?'

'The lower berth, No. 10.'

'And you had a companion?'

'Yes, a young English lady. Very nice, very amiable. She had travelled from Baghdad.'

'After the train left Vincovci, did she leave the compartment?'

'No, I am sure she did not.'

'Why are you sure if you were asleep?'

'I sleep very lightly. I am used to waking at a sound. I am sure if she had come down from the berth above I would have awakened.'

'Did you yourself leave the compartment?'

'Not until this morning.'

'Have you a scarlet silk kimono, Mademoiselle?'

'No, indeed. I have a good comfortable dressing-gown of Jaeger material.'

'A pale mauve abba such as you buy in the East.'

Poirot nodded. Then he said in a friendly tone:

'Why are you taking this journey? A holiday?'

'Yes, I am going home for a holiday. But first I go to Lausanne to stay with a sister for a week or so.'

'Perhaps you will be so amiable as to write me down the name and address of your sister?'

'With pleasure.'

She took the paper and pencil he gave her and wrote down the name and address as requested.

'Have you ever been in America, Mademoiselle?'

'No. Very nearly once. I was to go with an invalid lady, but it was cancelled at the last moment. I much regretted. They are very good, the Americans. They give much money to found schools and hospitals. They are very practical.'

'Do you remember hearing of the Armstrong kidnapping case?'

'No, what was that?'

Poirot explained.

Greta Ohlsson was indignant. Her yellow bun of hair quivered with her emotion.

'That there are in the world such evil men! It tries one's faith. The poor mother. My heart aches for her.'

The amiable Swede departed, her kindly face flushed, her eyes suffused with tears.

Poirot was writing busily on a sheet of paper.

'What is it you write there, my friend?' asked M. Bouc.

'*Mon cher*, it is my habit to be neat and orderly. I make here a little table of chronological events.'

He finished writing and passed the paper to M. Bouc.

9.15   Train leaves Belgrade.

about 9.40   Valet leaves Ratchett with sleeping draught beside him.

about 10.00   MacQueen leaves Ratchett.

about 10.40   Greta Ohlsson sees Ratchett (last seen alive).

N.B. – He was awake reading a book.

0.10   Train leaves Vincovci (late).

0.30   Train runs into a snowdrift.

0.37   Ratchett's bell rings. Conductor answers it. Ratchett says, '*Ce n'est rien. Je me suis trompé.*'

about 1.17   Mrs Hubbard thinks man is in her carriage. Rings for conductor.

M. Bouc nodded approval.

'That is very clear,' he said.

'There is nothing there that strikes you as at all odd?'

'No, it seems all quite clear and above board. It seems quite plain that the crime was committed at 1.15. The evidence of the watch shows us that, and Mrs Hubbard's story fits in. For my mind, I will make a guess at the identity of the murderer. I say, my friend, that it is the big Italian. He comes from America – from Chicago – and remember an Italian's weapon is the knife, and he stabs not once but several times.'

'That is true.'

'Without a doubt, that is the solution of the mystery. Doubtless he and this Ratchett were in this kidnapping business together. Cassetti is an Italian name. In some way Ratchett did on him what they call the double-cross. The Italian tracks him down, sends him warning letters first, and finally revenges himself upon him in a brutal way. It is all quite simple.'

Poirot shook his head doubtfully.

'It is hardly as simple as that, I fear,' he murmured.

'Me, I am convinced it is the truth,' said M. Bouc, becoming more and more enamoured of his theory.

'And what about the valet with the toothache who swears that the Italian never left the compartment?'

'That is the difficulty.'

Poirot twinkled.

'Yes, it is annoying, that. Unlucky for your theory, and extremely lucky for our Italian friend that M. Ratchett's valet should have had the toothache.'

'It will be explained,' said M. Bouc with magnificent certainty.

Poirot shook his head again.

'No, it is hardly so simple as that,' he murmured again.

Chapter 6

The Evidence of the Russian Princess

'Let us hear what Pierre Michel has to say about this button,' he said.

The Wagon Lit conductor was recalled. He looked at them inquiringly.

M. Bouc cleared his throat.

'Michel,' he said. 'Here is a button from your tunic. It was found in the American lady's compartment. What have you to say for yourself about it?'

The conductor's hand went automatically to his tunic.

'I have lost no button, Monsieur,' he said. 'There must be some mistake.'

'That is very odd.'

'I cannot account for it, Monsieur.'

The man seemed astonished, but not in any way guilty or confused.

M. Bouc said meaningly:

'Owing to the circumstances in which it was found, it seems fairly certain that this button was dropped by the man who was in Mrs Hubbard's compartment last night when she rang the bell.'

'But, Monsieur, there was no one there. The lady must have imagined it.'

'She did not imagine it, Michael. The assassin of M. Ratchett passed that way – *and dropped that button.*'

As the significance of M. Bouc's word became plain to him, Pierre Michel flew into a violent state of agitation.

'It is not true, Monsieur, it is not true!' he cried. 'You are accusing me of the crime. Me? I am innocent. I am absolutely innocent. Why should I want to kill a Monsieur whom I have never seen before?'

'Where were you when Mrs Hubbard's bell rang?'

'I told you, Monsieur, in the next coach, talking to my colleague.'

'We will send for him.'

'Do so, Monsieur, I implore you, do so.'

The conductor of the next coach was summoned. He immediately confirmed Pierre Michel's statement. He added that the conductor from the Bucharest coach had also been there. The three of them had been discussing the situation caused by the snow. They had been talking some ten minutes when Michel fancied he heard a bell. As he opened the doors connecting the two coaches, they had all heard it plainly. A bell ringing repeatedly. Michel had run post-haste to answer it.

'So you see, Monsieur, I am not guilty,' cried Michel anxiously.

'And this button from a Wagon Lit tunic – how do you explain it?'

'I cannot, Monsieur. It is a mystery to me. All my buttons are intact.'

Both of the other conductors also declared that they had not lost a button. Also that they had not been inside Mrs Hubbard's compartment at any time.

'Calm yourself, Michel,' said M. Bouc, 'and cast your mind back to the moment when you ran to answer Mrs Hubbard's bell. Did you meet anyone at all in the corridor?'

'No, Monsieur.'

'Did you see anyone going away from you down the corridor in the other direction?'

'Again, no. Monsieur.'

'Odd,' said M. Bouc.

'Not so very,' said Poirot. 'It is a question of time. Mrs Hubbard wakes to find someone in her compartment. For a minute or two she lies paralysed, her eyes shut. Probably it was then that the man slipped out into the corridor. Then she starts ringing the bell. But the conductor does not come at once. It is only the third or fourth peal that he hears. I should say myself that there was ample time –'

'For what? For what, *mon cher*? Remember that there are thick drifts of snow all round the train.'

'There are two courses open to our mysterious assassin,' said Poirot slowly. 'He could retreat into either of the toilets or he could disappear into one of the compartments.'

'But they were all occupied.'

'Yes.'

'You mean that he could retreat into his *own* compartment?'

Poirot nodded.

'It fits, it fits,' murmured M. Bouc. 'During that ten minutes' absence of the conductor, the murderer comes from his own compartment, goes into Ratchett's, kills him, locks and chains the door on the inside, goes out through Mrs Hubbard's compartment and is back safely in his own compartment by the time the conductor arrives.'

Poirot murmured:

'It is not quite so simple as that, my friend. Our friend the doctor here will tell you so.'

With a gesture M. Bouc signified that the three conductors might depart.

'We have still to see eight passengers,' said Poirot.

'Five first-class passengers – Princess Dragomiroff, Count and Countess Andrenyi, Colonel Arbuthnot and Mr Hardman. Three second-class passengers – Miss Debenham, Antonio Foscarelli and the lady's-maid, Fräulein Schmidt.'

'Who will you see first – the Italian?'

'How you harp on your Italian! No, we will start at the top of the tree. Perhaps Madame la Princesse will be so good as to spare us a few moments of her time. Convey that message to her, Michel.'

'*Oui, Monsieur*,' said the conductor, who was just leaving the car.

'Tell her we can wait on her in her compartment if she does not wish to put herself to the trouble of coming here,' called M. Bouc.

But Princess Dragomiroff declined to take this course. She appeared in the dining-car, inclined her head slightly and sat down opposite Poirot.

Her small toad-like face looked even yellower than the day before. She was certainly ugly, and yet, like the toad, she had eyes like jewels, dark and imperious, revealing latent energy and an intellectual force that could be felt at once.

Her voice was deep, very distinct, with a slight grating quality in it.

She cut short a flowery phrase of apology from M. Bouc.

'You need not offer apologies, Messieurs. I understand a murder has taken place. Naturally, you must interview all the passengers. I shall be glad to give all the assistance in my power.'

'You are most amiable, Madame,' said Poirot.

'Not at all. It is a duty. What do you wish to know?'

'Your full Christian names and address, Madame. Perhaps you would prefer to write them yourself?'

Poirot proffered a sheet of paper and pencil, but the Princess waved them aside.

'You can write it,' she said. 'There is nothing difficult – Natalia Dragomiroff, 17 Avenue Kleber, Paris.'

'You are travelling home from Constantinople, Madame?'

'Yes, I have been staying at the Austrian Embassy. My maid is with me.'

'Would you be so good as to give me a brief account of your movements last night from dinner onwards?'

'Willingly. I directed the conductor to make up my bed whilst I was in the dining-car. I retired to bed immediately after dinner. I read until the hour of eleven, when I turned out my light. I was unable to sleep owing to certain rheumatic pains from which I suffer. At about a quarter to one I rang for my maid. She massaged me and then read aloud till I felt sleepy. I cannot say exactly when she left me.

It may have been half an hour, it may have been later.'

'The train had stopped then?'

'The train had stopped.'

'You heard nothing – nothing unusual during the time, Madame?'

'I heard nothing unusual.'

'What is your maid's name?'

'Hildegarde Schmidt.'

'She has been with you long?'

'Fifteen years.'

'You consider her trustworthy?'

'Absolutely. Her people come from an estate of my late husband's in Germany.'

'You have been in America, I presume, Madame?'

The abrupt change of subject made the old lady raise her eyebrows.

'Many times.'

'Were you at any time acquainted with a family of the name of Armstrong – a family in which a tragedy occurred?'

With some emotion in her voice the old lady said:

'You speak of friends of mine, Monsieur.'

'You knew Colonel Armstrong well, then?'

'I knew him slightly; but his wife, Sonia Armstrong, was my god-daughter. I was on terms of friendship with her mother, the actress, Linda Arden. Linda Arden was a great genius, one of the greatest tragic actresses in the world. As Lady Macbeth, as Magda, there was no one to touch her. I was not only an admirer of her art, I was a personal friend.'

'She is dead?'

'No, no, she is alive, but she lives in complete retirement. Her health is very delicate, she has to lie on a sofa most of the time.'

'There was, I think, a second daughter?'

'Yes, much younger than Mrs Armstrong.'

'And she is alive?'

'Certainly.'

'Where is she?'

The old woman bent an acute glance at him.

'I must ask you the reason of these questions. What have they to do with the matter in hand – the murder on this train?'

'They are connected in this way, Madame, the man who was murdered was the man responsible for the kidnapping and murder of Mrs Armstrong's child.'

'Ah!'

The straight brows drew together. Princess Dragomiroff drew herself a little more erect.

'In my view, then, this murder is an entirely admirable happening! You will pardon my slightly biased point of view.'

'It is most natural, Madame. And now to return

156

to the question you did not answer. Where is the younger daughter of Linda Arden, the sister of Mrs Armstrong?'

'I honestly cannot tell you, Monsieur. I have lost touch with the younger generation. I believe she married an Englishman some years ago and went to England, but at the moment I cannot recollect the name.'

She paused a minute and then said:

'Is there anything further you want to ask me, gentlemen?'

'Only one thing, Madame, a somewhat personal question. The colour of your dressing-gown.'

She raised her eyebrows slightly.

'I must suppose you have a reason for such a question. My dressing-gown is of blue satin.'

'There is nothing more, Madame. I am much obliged to you for answering my questions so promptly.'

She made a slight gesture with her heavily-beringed hand.

Then, as she rose, and the others rose with her, she stopped.

'You will excuse me, Monsieur,' she said, 'but may I ask your name? Your face is somehow familiar to me.'

'My name, Madame, is Hercule Poirot – at your service.'

She was silent a minute, then:

'Hercule Poirot,' she said. 'Yes. I remember now. This is Destiny.'

She walked away, very erect, a little stiff in her movements.

'*Voilà une grande dame*,' said M. Bouc. 'What do you think of her, my friend?'

But Hercule Poirot merely shook his head.

'I am wondering,' he said, 'what she meant by Destiny.'

Chapter 7

The Evidence of Count and Countess Andrenyi

Count and Countess Andrenyi were next summoned. The Count, however, entered the dining-car alone.

There was no doubt that he was a fine-looking man seen face to face. He was at least six feet in height, with broad shoulders and slender hips. He was dressed in very well-cut English tweeds, and might have been taken for an Englishman had it not been for the length of his moustache and something in the line of the cheek-bone.

'Well, Messieurs,' he said, 'what can I do for you?'

'You understand, Monsieur,' said Poirot, 'that in view of what has occurred I am obliged to put certain questions to all the passengers.'

'Perfectly, perfectly,' said the Count easily. 'I quite understand your position. Not, I fear, that my wife and I can do much to assist you. We were asleep and heard nothing at all.'

'Are you aware of the identity of the deceased, Monsieur?'

'I understand it was the big American – a man with a decidedly unpleasant face. He sat at the table at meal times.'

He indicated with a nod of his head the table at which Ratchett and MacQueen had sat.

'Yes, yes, Monsieur, you are perfectly correct. I meant did you know the name of the man?'

'No.' The Count looked thoroughly puzzled by Poirot's queries.

'If you want to know his name,' he said, 'surely it is on his passport?'

'The name on his passport is Ratchett,' said Poirot. 'But that, Monsieur, is not his real name. He is the man Cassetti, who was responsible for a celebrated kidnapping outrage in America.'

He watched the Count closely as he spoke, but the latter seemed quite unaffected by the piece of news. He merely opened his eyes a little.

'Ah!' he said. 'That certainly should throw light upon the matter. An extraordinary country America.'

'You have been there, perhaps, Monsieur le Comte?'

'I was in Washington for a year.'

'You knew, perhaps, the Armstrong family?'

'Armstrong – Armstrong – it is difficult to recall – one met so many.'

He smiled, shrugged his shoulders.

'But to come back to the matter in hand, gentlemen,' he said. 'What more can I do to assist you?'

'You retired to rest – when, Monsieur le Comte?'

Hercule Poirot's eyes stole to his plan. Count and Countess Andrenyi occupied compartments No. 12 and 13 adjoining.

'We had one compartment made up for the night whilst we were in the dining-car. On returning we sat in the other for a while –'

'What number would that be?'

'No. 13. We played picquet together. About eleven o'clock my wife retired for the night. The conductor made up my compartment and I also went to bed. I slept soundly until morning.'

'Did you notice the stopping of the train?'

'I was not aware of it till this morning.'

'And your wife?'

The Count smiled.

'My wife always takes a sleeping draught when travelling by train. She took her usual dose of trional.'

He paused.

'I am sorry I am not able to assist you in any way.'

Poirot passed him a sheet of paper and a pen.

'Thank you, Monsieur le Comte. It is a formality, but will you just let me have your name and address?'

The Count wrote slowly and carefully.

'It is just as well I should write this for you,' he said pleasantly. 'The spelling of my country estate is a little difficult for those unacquainted with the language.'

He passed the paper across to Poirot and rose.

'It will be quite unnecessary for my wife to come here,' he said. 'She can tell you nothing more than I have.'

A little gleam came into Poirot's eye.

'Doubtless, doubtless,' he said. 'But all the same I think I should like to have just one little word with Madame la Comtesse.'

'I assure you it is quite unnecessary.'

His voice rang out authoritatively.

Poirot blinked gently at him.

'It will be a mere formality,' he said. 'But you understand, it is necessary for my report.'

'As you please.'

The Count gave way grudgingly. He made a short, foreign bow and left the dining-car.

Poirot reached out a hand to a passport. It set out the Count's name and titles. He passed on to the further information – *accompanied by wife*. Christian name Elena Maria; maiden name Goldenberg; age twenty. A spot of grease had been dropped some time by a careless official on it.

'A diplomatic passport,' said M. Bouc. 'We must be

careful, my friend, to give no offence. These people can have nothing to do with the murder.'

'Be easy, *mon vieux*, I will be most tactful. A mere formality.'

His voice dropped as the Countess Andrenyi entered the dining-car. She looked timid and extremely charming.

'You wish to see me, Messieurs?'

'A mere formality, Madame la Comtesse.' Poirot rose gallantly, bowed her into the seat opposite him. 'It is only to ask you if you saw or heard anything last night that may throw light upon this matter.'

'Nothing at all, Monsieur. I was asleep.'

'You did not hear, for instance, a commotion going on in the compartment next to yours? The American lady who occupies it had quite an attack of hysterics and rang for the conductor.'

'I heard nothing, Monsieur. You see, I had taken a sleeping draught.'

'Ah! I comprehend. Well, I need not detain you further.' Then, as she rose swiftly, 'Just one little minute – these particulars, your maiden name, age and so on, they are correct?'

'Quite correct, Monsieur.'

'Perhaps you will sign this memorandum to that effect, then.'

She signed quickly, a graceful slanting handwriting.

Elena Andrenyi.

'Did you accompany your husband to America, Madame?'

'No, Monsieur.' She smiled, flushed a little. 'We were not married then; we have only been married a year.'

'Ah yes, thank you, Madame. By the way, does your husband smoke?'

She stared at him as she stood poised for departure. 'Yes.'

'A pipe?'

'No. Cigarettes and cigars.'

'Ah! Thank you.'

She lingered; her eyes watched him curiously. Lovely eyes they were, dark and almond shaped, with very long black lashes that swept the exquisite pallor of her cheeks. Her lips, very scarlet, in the foreign fashion, were parted just a little. She looked exotic and beautiful.

'Why did you ask me that?'

'Madame,' Poirot waved an airy hand, 'detectives have to ask all sorts of questions. For instance, perhaps you will tell me the colour of your dressing-gown?'

She stared at him. Then she laughed.

'It is corn-coloured chiffon. Is that really important?'

'Very important, Madame.'

She asked curiously:

'Are you really a detective, then?'

'At your service, Madame.'

'I thought there were no detectives on the train when it passed through Yugo-Slavia – not until one got to Italy.'

'I am not a Yugo-Slavian detective, Madame. I am an international detective.'

'You belong to the League of Nations?'

'I belong to the world, Madame,' said Poirot dramatically. He went on, 'I work mainly in London. You speak English?' he added in that language.

'I speak a leetle, yes.'

Her accent was charming.

Poirot bowed once more.

'We will not detain you further, Madame. You see, it was not so very terrible.'

She smiled, inclined her head and departed.

'*Elle est jolie femme*,' said M. Bouc appreciatively.

He sighed.

'Well, that did not advance us much.'

'No,' said Poirot. 'Two people who saw nothing and heard nothing.'

'Shall we now see the Italian?'

Poirot did not reply for a moment. He was studying a grease spot on a Hungarian diplomatic passport.

Chapter 8

The Evidence of Colonel Arbuthnot

Poirot roused himself with a slight start. His eyes twinkled a little as they met the eager ones of M. Bouc.

'Ah! my dear old friend,' he said. 'You see, I have become what they call the snob! The first-class, I feel it should be attended to before the second-class. Next, I think, we will interview the good-looking Colonel Arbuthnot.'

Finding the Colonel's French to be of a severely limited description, Poirot conducted his interrogation in English.

Arbuthnot's name, age, home address and exact military standing were all ascertained. Poirot proceeded:

'It is that you come home from India on what is called the leave – what we call *en permission?*'

Colonel Arbuthnot, uninterested in what a pack of foreigners called anything, replied with true British brevity:

'Yes.'

'But you do not come home on the P. & O. boat?'

'No.'

'Why not?'

'I chose to come by the overland route for reasons of my own.'

'And that,' his manner seemed to say, 'is one for you, you interfering little jackanapes.'

'You came straight through from India?'

The Colonel replied dryly:

'I stopped for one night to see Ur of the Chaldees and for three days in Baghdad with the A.O.C., who happens to be an old friend of mine.'

'You stopped three days in Baghdad. I understand that the young English lady, Miss Debenham, also comes from Baghdad. Perhaps you met her there?'

'No, I did not. I first met Miss Debenham when she and I shared the railway convoy car from Kirkuk to Nissibin.'

Poirot leaned forward. He became persuasive and a little more foreign than he need have been.

'Monsieur, I am about to appeal to you. You and Miss Debenham are the only two English people on the train. It is necessary that I should ask you each your opinion of the other.'

'Highly irregular,' said Colonel Arbuthnot coldly.

'Not so. You see, this crime, it was most probably

committed by a woman. The man was stabbed no less than twelve times. Even the *chef de train* said at once, "It is a woman." Well, then, what is my first task? To give all the women travelling on the Stamboul-Calais coach what Americans call the "once over." But to judge of an Englishwoman is difficult. They are very reserved, the English. So I appeal to you, Monsieur, in the interests of justice. What sort of a person is this Miss Debenham? What do you know about her?'

'Miss Debenham,' said the Colonel with some warmth, 'is a lady.'

'Ah!' said Poirot with every appearance of being much gratified. 'So you do not think that she is likely to be implicated in this crime?'

'The idea is absurd,' said Arbuthnot. 'The man was a perfect stranger – she had never seen him before.'

'Did she tell you so?'

'She did. She commented at once upon his somewhat unpleasant appearance. If a woman *is* concerned, as you seem to think (to my mind without any evidence but mere assumption), I can assure you that Miss Debenham could not possibly be indicated.'

'You feel warmly in the matter,' said Poirot with a smile.

Colonel Arbuthnot gave him a cold stare.

'I really don't know what you mean,' he said.

The stare seemed to abash Poirot. He dropped

169

his eyes and began fiddling with the papers in front of him.

'All this is by the way,' he said. 'Let us be practical and come to facts. This crime, we have reason to believe, took place at a quarter-past one last night. It is part of the necessary routine to ask everyone on the train what he or she was doing at that time.'

'Quite so. At a quarter-past one, to the best of my belief, I was talking to the young American fellow – secretary to the dead man.'

'Ah! Were you in his compartment, or was he in yours?'

'I was in his.'

'That is the young man of the name of MacQueen?'

'Yes.'

'He was a friend or acquaintance of yours?'

'No, I never saw him before this journey. We fell into casual conversation yesterday and both became interested. I don't as a rule like Americans – haven't any use for 'em –'

Poirot smiled, remembering MacQueen's strictures on 'Britishers.'

'– But I liked this young fellow. He'd got hold of some tomfool idiotic ideas about the situation in India; that's the worst of Americans – they're so sentimental and idealistic. Well, he was interested in what I had to tell him. I've had nearly thirty years experience of the country. And I was interested in what he had to tell me about the financial situation in America. Then we got down to world politics in general. I was quite surprised to look at my watch and find it was a quarter to two.'

'That is the time you broke up this conversation?'

'Yes.'

'What did you do then?'

'Walked along to my own compartment and turned in.'

'Your bed was made up ready?'

'Yes.'

'That is the compartment – let me see – No. 15 – the one next but one to the end away from the dining-car?'

'Yes.'

'Where was the conductor when you went to your compartment?'

'Sitting at the end at a little table. As a matter of fact, MacQueen called him just as I went to my own compartment.'

'Why did he call him?'

'To make up his bed, I suppose. The compartment hadn't been made up for the night.'

'Now, Colonel Arbuthnot, I want you to think carefully. During the time you were talking to Mr MacQueen did anyone pass along the corridor outside the door?'

'A good many people, I should think. I wasn't paying attention.'

'Ah! but I am referring to – let us say the last hour and a half of your conversation. You got out at Vincovci, didn't you?'

'Yes, but only for about a minute. There was a blizzard on. The cold was something frightful. Made one quite thankful to get back to the fug, though as a rule I think the way these trains are overheated is something scandalous.'

M. Bouc sighed.

'It is very difficult to please everybody,' he said. 'The English, they open everything – then others, they come along and shut everything. It is very difficult.'

Neither Poirot nor Colonel Arbuthnot paid any attention to him.

'Now, Monsieur, cast your mind back,' said Poirot encouragingly. 'It was cold outside. You have returned to the train. You sit down again, you smoke – perhaps a cigarette, perhaps a pipe –'

He paused for the fraction of a second.

'A pipe for me. MacQueen smoked cigarettes.'

'The train starts again. You smoke your pipe. You discuss the state of Europe – of the world. It is late now. Most people have retired for the night. Does anyone pass the door – think?'

Arbuthnot frowned in the effort of remembrance.

'Difficult to say,' he said. 'You see, I wasn't paying any attention.'

'But you have the soldier's observation for detail. You notice without noticing, so to speak.'

The Colonel thought again, but shook his head.

'I couldn't say. I don't remember anyone passing except the conductor. Wait a minute – and there was a woman, I think.'

'You saw her? Was she old – young?'

'Didn't see her. Wasn't looking that way. Just a rustle and a sort of smell of scent.'

'Scent? A *good* scent?'

'Well, rather fruity, if you know what I mean. I mean you'd smell it a hundred yards away. But mind you,' the Colonel went on hastily, 'this may have been earlier in the evening. You see, as you said just now, it was just one of those things you notice without noticing, so to speak. Some time that evening I said to myself, "Woman – scent – got it on pretty thick." But *when* it was I can't be sure, except that – why, yes, it must have been after Vincovci.'

'Why?'

'Because I remember – sniffing, you know – just when I was talking about the utter washout Stalin's Five Year Plan was turning out. I know the idea – woman – brought the idea of the position of women in Russia into my mind. And I know we hadn't got on to Russia until pretty near the end of our talk.'

'You can't pin it down more definitely than that?'

'N-no. It must have been roughly within the last half-hour.'

'It was after the train had stopped?'

The other nodded.

'Yes, I'm almost sure it was.'

'Well, we will pass from that. Have you ever been in America, Colonel Arbuthnot?'

'Never. Don't want to go.'

'Did you ever know a Colonel Armstrong?'

'Armstrong – Armstrong – I've known two or three Armstrongs. There was Tommy Armstrong in the 60th – you don't mean him? And Selby Armstrong – he was killed on the Somme.'

'I mean the Colonel Armstrong who married an American wife and whose only child was kidnapped and killed.'

'Ah, yes, I remember reading about that – shocking affair. I don't think I actually ever came across the fellow, though, of course, I knew of him. Toby Armstrong. Nice fellow. Everybody liked him. He had a very distinguished career. Got the V.C.'

'The man who was killed last night was the man responsible for the murder of Colonel Armstrong's child.'

Arbuthnot's face grew rather grim.

'Then in my opinion the swine deserved what he got. Though I would have preferred to have seen him properly hanged – or electrocuted, I suppose, over there.'

'In fact, Colonel Arbuthnot, you prefer law and order to private vengeance?'

'Well, you can't go about having blood feuds and stabbing each other like Corsicans or the Mafia,' said the Colonel. 'Say what you like, trial by jury is a sound system.'

Poirot looked at him thoughtfully for a minute or two.

'Yes,' he said. 'I am sure that would be your view. Well, Colonel Arbuthnot, I do not think there is anything more I have to ask you. There is nothing you yourself can recall last night that in any way struck you – or shall we say strikes you now looking back – as suspicious?'

Arbuthnot considered for a moment or two.

'No,' he said. 'Nothing at all. Unless –' he hesitated.

'But yes, continue, I pray of you.'

'Well, it's nothing really,' said the Colonel slowly. 'But you said *anything*.'

'Yes, yes. Go on.'

'Oh, it's nothing. A mere detail. But as I got back

175

to my compartment I noticed that the door of the one beyond mine – the end one, you know –'

'Yes, No. 16.'

'Well, the door of it was not quite closed. And the fellow inside peered out in a furtive sort of way. Then he pulled the door to quickly. Of course, I know there's nothing in that – but it just struck me as a bit odd. I mean, it's quite usual to open a door and stick your head out if you want to see anything. But it was the furtive way he did it that caught my attention.'

'Ye-es,' said Poirot doubtfully.

'I told you there was nothing to it,' said Arbuthnot apologetically. 'But you know what it is – early hours of the morning – everything very still – the thing had a sinister look – like a detective story. All non-sense, really.'

He rose.

'Well, if you don't want me any more –'

'Thank you, Colonel Arbuthnot, there is nothing else.'

The soldier hesitated for a minute. His first natural distaste for being questioned by 'foreigners' had evaporated.

'About Miss Debenham,' he said rather awkwardly. 'You can take it from me that she's all right. She's a *pukka sahib*.'

Flushing a little, he withdrew.

'What,' asked Dr Constantine with interest, 'does a *pukka sahib* mean?'

'It means,' said Poirot, 'that Miss Debenham's father and brothers were at the same kind of school as Colonel Arbuthnot.'

'Oh!' said Dr Constantine, disappointed. 'Then it has nothing to do with the crime at all.'

'Exactly,' said Poirot.

He fell into a reverie, beating a light tattoo on the table. Then he looked up.

'Colonel Arbuthnot smokes a pipe,' he said. 'In the compartment of M. Ratchett I found a pipe-cleaner. M. Ratchett smoked only cigars.'

'You think –?'

'He is the only man so far who admits to smoking a pipe. And he knew of Colonel Armstrong – perhaps actually did know him though he won't admit it.'

'So you think it possible –'

Poirot shook his head violently.

'That is just it – it is *im*possible – quite impossible – that an honourable, slightly stupid, upright Englishman should stab an enemy twelve times with a knife! Do you not feel, my friends, how impossible it is?'

'That is the psychology,' said M. Bouc.

'And one must respect the psychology. This crime has a signature and it is certainly not the signature

177

of Colonel Arbuthnot. But now to our next interview.'

This time M. Bouc did not mention the Italian. But he thought of him.

Chapter 9

The Evidence of Mr Hardman

The last of the first-class passengers to be interviewed – Mr Hardman – was the big flamboyant American who had shared a table with the Italian and the valet.

He wore a somewhat loud check suit, a pink shirt, a flashy tiepin, and was rolling something round his tongue as he entered the dining-car. He had a big, fleshy, coarse-featured face, with a good-humoured expression.

'Morning, gentlemen,' he said. 'What can I do for you?'

'You have heard of this murder, Mr – er – Hardman?'

'Sure.'

He shifted the chewing gum deftly.

'We are of necessity interviewing all the passengers on the train.'

'That's all right by me. Guess that's the only way to tackle the job.'

179

Poirot consulted the passport lying in front of him.

'You are Cyrus Bethman Hardman, United States subject, forty-one years of age, travelling salesman for typewriting ribbons?'

'O.K., that's me.'

'You are travelling from Stamboul to Paris?'

'That's so.'

'Reason?'

'Business.'

'Do you always travel first-class, Mr Hardman?'

'Yes, sir. The firm pays my travelling expenses.'

He winked.

'Now, Mr Hardman, we come to the events of last night.'

The American nodded.

'What can you tell us about the matter?'

'Exactly nothing at all.'

'Ah, that is a pity. Perhaps, Mr Hardman, you will tell us exactly what you did last night, from dinner onwards?'

For the first time the American did not seem ready with his reply. At last he said:

'Excuse me, gentlemen, but just who are you? Put me wise.'

'This is M. Bouc, a director of the Compagnie des Wagons Lits. This gentleman is the doctor who examined the body.'

'And you yourself?'

'I am Hercule Poirot. I am engaged by the company to investigate this matter.'

'I've heard of you,' said Mr Hardman. He reflected a minute or two longer. 'Guess I'd better come clean.'

'It will certainly be advisable for you to tell us all you know,' said Poirot dryly.

'You'd have said a mouthful if there was anything I *did* know. But I don't. I know nothing at all – just as I said. But I *ought* to know something. That's what makes me sore. I *ought* to.'

'Please explain, Mr Hardman.'

Mr Hardman sighed, removed the chewing gum, and dived into a pocket. At the same time his whole personality seemed to undergo a change. He became less of a stage character and more of a real person. The resonant nasal tones of his voice became modified.

'That passport's a bit of bluff,' he said. 'That's who I really am.'

Poirot scrutinized the card flipped across to him. M. Bouc peered over his shoulder.

Mr Cyrus B. Hardman
McNeil's Detective Agency,
New York.

Poirot knew the name. It was one of the best known

181

and most reputable private detective agencies in New York.

'Now, Mr Hardman,' he said. 'Let us hear the meaning of this.'

'Sure. Things came about this way. I'd come over to Europe trailing a couple of crooks – nothing to do with this business. The chase ended in Stamboul. I wired the Chief and got his instructions to return, and I would have been making my tracks back to little old New York when I got this.'

He pushed across a letter.

The heading at the top was the Tokatlian Hotel.

Dear Sir, – You have been pointed out to me as an operative of the McNeil Detective Agency. Kindly report to my suite at four o'clock this afternoon.

It was signed 'S.E. Ratchett.'

'*Eh bien?*'

'I reported at the time stated and Mr Ratchett put me wise to the situation. He showed me a couple of letters he'd got.'

'He was alarmed?'

'Pretended not to be, but he was rattled all right. He put up a proposition to me. I was to travel by the same train as he did to Parrus and see that nobody got him. Well, gentlemen, I *did* travel by the same train and, in spite of me, somebody *did* get him. I certainly feel sore about it. It doesn't look any too good for me.'

'Did he give you any indication of the line you were to take?'

'Sure. He had it all taped out. It was his idea that I should travel in the compartment alongside his – well, that was blown upon straight away. The only place I could get was berth No. 16, and I had a bit of a job getting that. I guess the conductor likes to keep that compartment up his sleeve. But that's neither here nor there. When I looked all round the situation, it seemed to me that No. 16 was a pretty good strategic position. There was only the dining-car in front of the Stamboul sleeping-car, the door on to the platform at the front end was barred at night. The only way a thug could come was through the rear end door to the platform or along the train from the rear – in either case he'd have to pass right by my compartment.'

'You had no idea, I suppose, of the identity of the possible assailant.'

'Well, I knew what he looked like. Mr Ratchett described him to me.'

'What?'

All three men leaned forward eagerly.

Hardman went on:

'A small man, dark, with a womanish kind of voice – that's what the old man said. Said, too, that he didn't think it would be the first night out. More likely the second or third.'

'He knew something,' said M. Bouc.

'He certainly knew more than he told his secretary,' said Poirot thoughtfully. 'Did he tell you anything about this enemy of his? Did he, for instance, say *why* his life was threatened?'

'No, he was kinder reticent about that part of it. Just said the fellow was out for his blood and meant to get it.'

'A small man – dark – with a womanish voice,' said Poirot thoughtfully.

Then, fixing a sharp glance on Hardman, he said:

'You knew who he really was, of course?'

'Which, mister?'

'Ratchett. You recognized him?'

'I don't get you.'

'Ratchett was Cassetti, the Armstrong murderer.'

Mr Hardman gave way to a prolonged whistle.

'That certainly is some surprise!' he said. 'Yes, *sir*! No, I didn't recognize him. I was away out West when that case came on. I suppose I saw photos of him in the papers, but I wouldn't recognize my own mother when a press photographer had done with her. Well, I don't doubt that a few people had it in for Cassetti all right.'

'Do you know of anyone connected with the

Armstrong case who answers to that description –
small, dark, womanish voice?'

Hardman reflected a minute or two.

'It's hard to say. Pretty nearly everyone to do with
that case is dead.'

'There was the girl who threw herself out of the
window, remember.'

'Sure. That's a good point, that. She was a foreigner
of some kind. Maybe she had some wop relations. But
you've got to remember that there were other cases
besides the Armstrong case. Cassetti had been running
this kidnapping stunt some time. You can't concentrate
on that only.'

'Ah, but we have reason to believe that this crime is
connected with the Armstrong case.'

Mr Hardman cocked an inquiring eye. Poirot did not
respond. The American shook his head.

'I can't call to mind anybody answering that description in the Armstrong case,' he said slowly. 'But of
course I wasn't in it and didn't know much about it.'

'Well, continue your narrative, M. Hardman.'

'There's very little to tell. I got my sleep in the day-
time and stayed awake on the watch at night. Nothing
suspicious happened the first night. Last night was the
same, as far as I was concerned. I had my door a little
ajar and watched. No stranger passed.'

'You are sure of that, M. Hardman?'

'I'm plumb certain. Nobody got on that train from outside and nobody came along the train from the rear carriages. I'll take my oath on that.'

'Could you see the conductor from your position?'

'Sure. He sits on that little seat almost flush with my door.'

'Did he leave that seat at all after the train stopped at Vincovci?'

'That was the last station? Why, yes, he answered a couple of bells – that would be just after the train came to a halt for good. Then, after that, he went past me into the rear coach – was there about a quarter of an hour. There was a bell ringing like mad and he came back running. I stepped out into the corridor to see what it was all about – felt a mite nervous, you understand – but it was only the American dame. She was raising hell about something or other. I grinned. Then he went on to another compartment and came back and got a bottle of mineral water for someone. After that he settled down in his seat till he went up to the far end to make somebody's bed up. I don't think he stirred after that until about five o'clock this morning.'

'Did he doze off at all?'

'That I can't say. He may have done.'

Poirot nodded. Automatically his hands straightened the papers on the table. He picked up the official card once more.

'Be so good as just to initial this,' he said.

The other complied.

'There is no one, I suppose, who can confirm your story of your identity, M. Hardman?'

'On this train? Well, not exactly. Unless it might be young MacQueen. I know him well enough – seen him in his father's office in New York – but that's not to say he'll remember me from a crowd of other operatives. No, Mr Poirot, you'll have to wait and cable New York when the snow lets up. But it's O.K. I'm not telling the tale. Well, so long, gentlemen. Pleased to have met you, Mr Poirot.'

Poirot proffered his cigarette case.

'But perhaps you prefer a pipe?'

'Not me.'

He helped himself, then strode briskly off.

The three men looked at each other.

'You think he is genuine?' asked Dr Constantine.

'Yes, yes. I know the type. Besides, it is a story that would be very easily disproved.'

'He has given us a piece of very interesting evidence,' said M. Bouc.

'Yes, indeed.'

'A small man, dark, with a high-pitched voice,' said M. Bouc thoughtfully.

'A description which applies to no one on the train,' said Poirot.

Chapter 10

The Evidence of the Italian

'And now,' said Poirot with a twinkle in his eye, 'we will delight the heart of M. Bouc and see the Italian.'

Antonio Foscarelli came into the dining-car with a swift, cat-like tread. His face beamed. It was a typical Italian face, sunny looking and swarthy.

He spoke French well and fluently, with only a slight accent.

'Your name is Antonio Foscarelli?'

'Yes, Monsieur.'

'You are, I see, a naturalized American subject?'

The American grinned.

'Yes, Monsieur. It is better for my business.'

'You are an agent for Ford motor cars?'

'Yes, you see –'

A voluble exposition followed. At the end of it, anything that the three men did not know about Foscarelli's business methods, his journeys, his income,

Agatha Christie

and his opinion of the United States and most European countries seemed a negligible factor. This was not a man who had to have information dragged from him. It gushed out.

His good-natured childish face beamed with satisfaction as with a last eloquent gesture, he paused and wiped his forehead with a handkerchief.

'So you see,' he said, 'I do big business. I am up to date. I understand salesmanship!'

'You have been in the United States, then, for the last ten years on and off?'

'Yes, Monsieur. Ah! well do I remember the day I first took the boat – to go to America, so far away! My mother, my little sister –'

Poirot cut short the flood of reminiscence.

'During your sojourn in the United States did you ever come across the deceased?'

'Never. But I know the type. Oh, yes.' He snapped his fingers expressively. 'It is very respectable, very well dressed, but underneath it is all wrong. Out of my experience, I should say he was the big crook. I give you my opinion for what it is worth.'

'Your opinion is quite right,' said Poirot dryly. 'Ratchett was Cassetti, the kidnapper.'

'What did I tell you? I have learned to be very acute – to read the face. It is necessary. Only in America do they teach you the proper way to sell.'

'You remember the Armstrong case?

'I do not quite remember. The name, yes? It was a little girl – a baby – was it not?'

'Yes, a very tragic affair.'

The Italian seemed the first person to demur to this view.

'Ah, well, these things they happen,' he said philosophically, 'in a great civilization such as America –'

Poirot cut him short.

'Did you ever come across any members of the Armstrong family?'

'No, I do not think so. It is difficult to say. I will give you some figures. Last year alone I sold –'

'Monsieur, pray confine yourself to the point.'

The Italian's hands flung themselves out in a gesture of apology.

'A thousand pardons.'

'Tell me, if you please, your exact movements last night from dinner onwards.'

'With pleasure. I stay here as long as I can. It is more amusing. I talk to the American gentleman at my table. He sells typewriter ribbons. Then I go back to my compartment. It is empty. The miserable John Bull who shares it with me is away attending to his master. At last he comes back – very long face as usual. He will not talk – says yes and no. A miserable race, the English – not sympathetic. He sits in the corner, very stiff, reading a

191

book. Then the conductor comes and makes our beds.'

'Nos. 4 and 5,' murmured Poirot.

'Exactly – the end compartment. Mine is the upper berth. I get up there. I smoke and read. The little Englishman has, I think, the toothache. He gets out a little bottle of stuff that smells very strong. He lies in bed and groans. Presently I sleep. Whenever I wake I hear him groaning.'

'Do you know if he left the carriage at all during the night?'

'I do not think so. That, I should hear. The light from the corridor – one wakes up automatically thinking it is the Customs examination at some frontier.'

'Did he ever speak of his master? Ever express any animus against him?'

'I tell you he did not speak. He was not sympathetic. A fish.'

'You smoke, you say – a pipe, cigarettes, cigars?'

'Cigarettes only.'

Poirot proffered him one which he accepted.

'Have you ever been in Chicago?' inquired M. Bouc.

'Oh, yes – a fine city – but I know best New York, Washington, Detroit. You have been to the States? No? You should go, it –'

Poirot pushed a sheet of paper across to him.

'If you will sign this, and put your permanent address, please.'

The Italian wrote with a flourish. Then he rose – his smile was as engaging as ever.

'That is all? You do not require me further? Good-day to you, Messieurs. I wish we could get out of the snow. I have an appointment in Milan –' He shook his head sadly. 'I shall lose the business.'

He departed.

Poirot looked at his friend.

'He has been a long time in America,' said M. Bouc, 'and he is an Italian, and Italians use the knife! And they are great liars! I do not like Italians.'

'*Ça se voit*,' said Poirot with a smile. 'Well, it may be that you are right, but I will point out to you, my friend, that there is absolutely no evidence against the man.'

'And what about the psychology? Do not Italians stab?'

'Assuredly,' said Poirot. 'Especially in the heat of a quarrel. But this – this is a different kind of crime. I have the little idea, my friend, that this is a crime very carefully planned and staged. It is a far-sighted, long-headed crime. It is not – how shall I express it? – a *Latin* crime. It is a crime that shows traces of a cool, resourceful, deliberate brain – I think an Anglo-Saxon brain.'

He picked up the last two passports.

'Let us now,' he said, 'see Miss Mary Debenham.'

Chapter 11

The Evidence of Miss Debenham

When Mary Debenham entered the dining-car she confirmed Poirot's previous estimate of her.

Very neatly dressed in a little black suit with a French grey shirt, the smooth waves of her dark head were neat and unruffled. Her manner was as calm and unruffled as her hair.

She sat down opposite Poirot and M. Bouc and looked at them inquiringly.

'Your name is Mary Hermione Debenham, and you are twenty-six years of age?' began Poirot.

'Yes.'

'English?'

'Yes.'

'Will you be so kind, Mademoiselle, as to write down your permanent address on this piece of paper?'

She complied. Her writing was clear and legible.

'And now, Mademoiselle, what have you to tell us

of the affair last night?'

'I am afraid I have nothing to tell you. I went to bed and slept.'

'Does it distress you very much, Mademoiselle, that a crime has been committed on this train?'

The question was clearly unexpected. Her grey eyes widened a little.

'I don't quite understand you.'

'It was a perfectly simple question that I asked you, Mademoiselle. I will repeat it. Are you very much distressed that a crime should have been committed on this train?'

'I have not really thought about it from that point of view. No, I cannot say that I am at all distressed.'

'A crime – it is all in the day's work to you, eh?'

'It is naturally an unpleasant thing to have happen,' said Mary Debenham quietly.

'You are very Anglo-Saxon. Mademoiselle. *Vous n'éprouvez pas d'emotion.*'

She smiled a little.

'I am afraid I cannot have hysterics to prove my sensibility. After all, people die every day.'

'They die, yes. But murder is a little more rare.'

'Oh, certainly.'

'You were not acquainted with the dead man?'

'I saw him for the first time when lunching here yesterday.'

'And how did he strike you?'

'I hardly noticed him.'

'He did not strike you as an evil personality.'

She shrugged her shoulders slightly.

'Really, I cannot say I thought about it.'

Poirot looked at her keenly.

'You are, I think, a little bit contemptuous of the way I prosecute my inquiries,' he said with a twinkle. 'Not so, you think, would an English inquiry be conducted. There everything would be cut and dried – it would be all kept to the facts – a well-ordered business. But I, Mademoiselle, have my little originalities. I look first at my witness, I sum up his or her character, and I frame my questions accordingly. Just a little minute ago I am asking questions of a gentleman who wants to tell me all his ideas on every subject. Well, him I keep strictly to the point. I want him to answer yes or no, this or that. And then you come. I see at once that you will be orderly and methodical. You will confine yourself to the matter in hand. Your answers will be brief and to the point. And because, Mademoiselle, human nature is perverse, I ask of you quite different questions. I ask what you *feel*, what you *thought*. It does not please you this method?'

'If you will forgive my saying so, it seems somewhat of a waste of time. Whether or not I liked Mr Ratchett's face does not seem likely to be helpful in finding out who killed him.'

Agatha Christie

'Do you know who the man Ratchett really was, Mademoiselle?'

She nodded.

'Mrs Hubbard has been telling everyone.'

'And what do you think of the Armstrong affair?'

'It was quite abominable,' said the girl crisply.

Poirot looked at her thoughtfully.

'You are travelling from Baghdad, I believe, Miss Debenham?'

'Yes.'

'To London?'

'Yes.'

'What have you been doing in Baghdad?'

'I have been acting as governess to two children.'

'Are you returning to your post after your holiday?'

'I am not sure.'

'Why is that?'

'Baghdad is rather out of things. I think I should prefer a post in London if I can hear of a suitable one.'

'I see. I thought, perhaps, you might be going to be married.'

Miss Debenham did not reply. She raised her eyes and looked Poirot full in the face. The glance said plainly, 'You are impertinent.'

'What is your opinion of the lady who shares your compartment – Miss Ohlsson?'

'She seems a pleasant, simple creature.'

'What colour is her dressing-gown?'

Mary Debenham stared.

'A kind of brownish colour – natural wool.'

'Ah! I may mention without indiscretion, I hope, that I noticed the colour of your dressing-gown on the way from Aleppo to Stamboul. A pale mauve, I believe.'

'Yes, that is right.'

'Have you any other dressing-gown, Mademoiselle? A scarlet dressing-gown, for example?'

'No, that is not mine.'

Poirot leaned forward. He was like a cat pouncing on a mouse.

'Whose, then?'

The girl drew back a little, startled.

'I don't know. What do you mean?'

'You do not say, "No, I have no such thing." You say, "That is not mine" – meaning that such a thing *does* belong to someone else.'

She nodded.

'Somebody else on this train?'

'Yes.'

'Whose is it?'

'I told you just now. I don't know. I woke up this morning about five o'clock with the feeling that the train had been standing still for a long time. I opened the door and looked out into the corridor, thinking we might be at a station. I saw someone in a scarlet kimono some way down the corridor.'

'And you don't know who it was? Was she fair or dark or grey-haired?'

'I can't say. She had on a shingle cap and I only saw the back of her head.'

'And in build?'

'Tallish and slim, I should judge, but it's difficult to say. The kimono was embroidered with dragons.'

'Yes, yes that is right, dragons.'

He was silent a minute. He murmured to himself:

'I cannot understand. I cannot understand. None of this makes sense.'

Then, looking up, he said:

'I need not keep you further, Mademoiselle.'

'Oh!' she seemed rather taken aback, but rose promptly. In the doorway, however, she hesitated a minute and then came back.

'The Swedish lady – Miss Ohlsson, is it? – seems rather worried. She says you told her she was the last person to see this man alive. She thinks, I believe, that you suspect her on that account. Can't I tell her that she has made a mistake? Really, you know, she is the kind of creature who wouldn't hurt a fly.'

She smiled a little as she spoke.

'What time was it that she went to fetch the aspirin from Mrs Hubbard?'

'Just after half-past ten.'

'She was away – how long?'

'About five minutes.'

'Did she leave the compartment again during the night?'

'No.'

Poirot turned to the doctor.

'Could Ratchett have been killed as early as that?'

The doctor shook his head.

'Then I think you can reassure your friend, Mademoiselle.'

'Thank you.' She smiled suddenly at him, a smile that invited sympathy. 'She's like a sheep, you know. She gets anxious and bleats.'

She turned and went out.

Chapter 12

The Evidence of the German Lady's-Maid

M. Bouc was looking at his friend curiously.

'I do not quite understand you, *mon vieux*. You were trying to do – what?'

'I was searching for a flaw, my friend.'

'A flaw?'

'Yes – in the armour of a young lady's self-possession. I wished to shake her *sang-froid*. Did I succeed? I do not know. But I know this – she did not expect me to tackle the matter as I did.'

'You suspect her,' said M. Bouc slowly. 'But why? She seems a very charming young lady – the last person in the world to be mixed up in a crime of this kind.'

'I agree,' said Constantine. 'She is cold. She has not emotions. She would not stab a man; she would sue him in the law courts.'

Poirot sighed 'You must, both of you, get rid of

Agatha Christie

your obsession that this is an unpremeditated and sudden crime. As for the reason why I suspect Miss Debenham, there are two. One is because of something that I overheard, and that you do not as yet know.'

He retailed to them the curious interchange of phrases he had overheard on the journey from Aleppo.

'That is curious, certainly,' said M. Bouc when he had finished. 'It needs explaining. If it means what you suspect it means, then they are both of them in it together – she and the stiff Englishman.'

Poirot nodded.

'And that is just what is not borne out by the facts,' he said. 'See you, if they were both in this together, what should we expect to find – that each of them would provide an alibi for the other. Is not that so? But no – that does not happen. Miss Debenham's alibi is provided by a Swedish woman whom she has never seen before, and Colonel Arbuthnot's alibi is vouched for by MacQueen, the dead man's secretary. No, that solution of the puzzle is too easy.'

'You said there was another reason for your suspicions of her,' M. Bouc reminded him.

Poirot smiled.

'Ah! but that is only psychological. I ask myself, is it possible for Miss Debenham to have planned this crime? Behind this business, I am convinced, there is a cool, intelligent, resourceful brain. Miss Debenham answers to that description.'

M. Bouc shook his head.

'I think you are wrong, my friend. I do not see that young English girl as a criminal.'

'Ah, well,' said Poirot, picking up the last passport, 'to the final name on our list. Hildegarde Schmidt, lady's-maid.'

Summoned by the attendant, Hildegarde Schmidt came into the restaurant-car and stood waiting respectfully.

Poirot motioned her to sit down.

She did so, folding her hands and waiting placidly till he questioned her. She seemed a placid creature altogether – eminently respectable – perhaps not over intelligent.

Poirot's methods with Hildegarde Schmidt were a complete contrast to his handling of Mary Debenham.

He was at his kindest and most genial, setting the woman at her ease. Then, having got her to write down her name and address, he slid gently into his questions.

The interview took place in German.

'We want to know as much as possible about what happened last night,' he said. 'We know that you cannot give us much information bearing on the crime itself, but you may have seen or heard something that,

205

while conveying nothing to you, may be valuable to us. You understand?'

She did not seem to. Her broad, kindly face remained set in its expression of placid stupidity as she answered:

'I do not know anything, Monsieur.'

'Well, for instance, you know that your mistress sent for you last night?'

'That, yes.'

'Do you remember the time?'

'I do not, Monsieur. I was asleep, you see, when the attendant came and told me.'

'Yes, yes. Was it usual for you to be sent for in this way?'

'It was not unusual, Monsieur. The gracious lady often required attention at night. She did not sleep well.'

'*Eh bien*, then, you received the summons and you got up. Did you put on a dressing-gown?'

'No, Monsieur, I put on a few clothes. I would not like to go in to her Excellency in my dressing-gown.'

'And yet it is a very nice dressing-gown – scarlet, is it not?'

She stared at him.

'It is a dark-blue flannel dressing-gown, Monsieur.'

'Ah! continue. A little pleasantry on my part, that is all. So you went along to Madame la Princesse. And what did you do when you got there?'

'I gave her massage, Monsieur, and then I read aloud. I do not read aloud very well, but her Excellency says that is all the better. So it sends her better to sleep. When she became sleepy, Monsieur, she told me to go, so I closed the book and I returned to my own compartment.'

'Do you know what time that was?'

'No, Monsieur.'

'Well, how long had you been with Madame la Princesse?'

'About half an hour, Monsieur.'

'Good, continue.'

'First, I fetched her Excellency an extra rug from my compartment. It was very cold in spite of the heating. I arranged the rug over her and she wished me good-night. I poured her out some mineral water. Then I turned out the light and left her.'

'And then?'

'There is nothing more, Monsieur. I returned to my carriage and went to sleep.'

'And you met no one in the corridor?'

'No, Monsieur.'

'You did not, for instance, see a lady in a scarlet kimono with dragons on it?'

Her mild eyes bulged at him.

'No, indeed, Monsieur. There was nobody about except the attendant. Everyone was asleep.'

'But you did see the conductor?'

'Yes, Monsieur.'

'What was he doing?'

'He came out of one of the compartments, Monsieur.'

'What?' M. Bouc leaned forward. 'Which one?'

Hildegarde Schmidt looked frightened again and Poirot cast a reproachful glance at his friend.

'Naturally,' he said. 'The conductor often has to answer bells at night. Do you remember which compartment it was?'

'It was about the middle of the coach, Monsieur. Two or three doors from Madame la Princesse.'

'Ah! tell us, if you please, exactly where this was and what happened.'

'He nearly ran into me, Monsieur. It was when I was returning from my compartment to that of the Princess with the rug.'

'And he came out of a compartment and almost collided with you? In which direction was he going?'

'Towards me, Monsieur. He apologized and passed on down the corridor towards the dining-car. A bell began ringing, but I do not think he answered it.'

She paused and then said:

'I do not understand. How is it –?'

Poirot spoke reassuringly.

'It is just a question of times,' he said. 'All a matter

of routine. This poor conductor, he seems to have had a busy night – first waking you and then answering bells.'

'It was not the same conductor who woke me, Monsieur. It was another one.'

'Ah, another one! Had you seen him before?'

'No. Monsieur.'

'Ah! Do you think you would recognize him if you saw him?'

'I think so, Monsieur.'

Poirot murmured something in M. Bouc's ear. The latter got up and went to the door to give an order.

Poirot was continuing his questions in an easy friendly manner.

'Have you ever been to America, Frau Schmidt?'

'Never, Monsieur. It must be a fine country.'

'You have heard, perhaps, of who this man who was killed really was – that he was responsible for the death of a little child.'

'Yes, I have heard, Monsieur. It was abominable – wicked. The good God should not allow such things. We are not so wicked as that in Germany.'

Tears had come into the woman's eyes. Her strong motherly soul was moved.

'It was an abominable crime,' said Poirot gravely.

He drew a scrap of cambric from his pocket and handed it to her.

'Is this your handkerchief, Frau Schmidt?'

There was a moment's silence as the woman examined it. She looked up after a minute. The colour had mounted a little in her face.

'Ah! no, indeed. It is not mine, Monsieur.'

'It has the initial H, you see. That is why I thought it was yours.'

'Ah! Monsieur, it is a lady's handkerchief, that. A very expensive handkerchief. Embroidered by hand. It comes from Paris, I should say.'

'It is not yours and you do not know whose it is?'

'I? Oh, no, Monsieur.'

Of the three listening, only Poirot caught the nuance of hesitation in the reply.

M. Bouc whispered in his ear. Poirot nodded and said to the woman:

'The three sleeping-car attendants are coming in. Will you be so kind as to tell me which is the one you met last night as you were going with the rug to the Princess?'

The three men entered. Pierre Michel, the big blond conductor of the Athens-Paris coach, and the stout burly conductor of the Bucharest one.

Hildegarde Schmidt looked at them and immediately shook her head.

'No, Monsieur,' she said. 'None of these is the man I saw last night.'

'But these are the only conductors on the train. You must be mistaken.'

'I am quite sure, Monsieur. These are all tall, big men. The one I saw was small and dark. He had a little moustache. His voice when he said "*Pardon*" was weak like a woman's. Indeed, I remember him very well, Monsieur.'

Chapter 13

Summary of the Passengers' Evidence

'A small dark man with a womanish voice,' said M. Bouc.

The three conductors and Hildegarde Schmidt had been dismissed.

'But I understand nothing – but nothing of all this! The enemy that this Ratchett spoke of, he was then on the train after all? But where is he now? How can he have vanished into thin air? My head, it whirls. Say something, then, my friend, I implore you. Show me how the impossible can be possible!'

'It is a good phrase that,' said Poirot. 'The impossible cannot have happened, therefore the impossible must be possible in spite of appearances.'

'Explain to me then, quickly, what actually happened on the train last night.'

'I am not a magician, *mon cher*. I am, like you, a very

puzzled man. This affair advances in a very strange manner.'

'It does not advance at all. It stays where it was.'

Poirot shook his head.

'No, that is not true. We are more advanced. We know certain things. We have heard the evidence of the passengers.'

'And what has that told us? Nothing at all.'

'I would not say that, my friend.'

'I exaggerate, perhaps. The American, Hardman, and the German maid – yes, they have added some-thing to our knowledge. That is to say, they have made the whole business more unintelligible than it was.'

'No, no, no,' said Poirot soothingly.

M. Bouc turned upon him.

'Speak, then, let us hear the wisdom of Hercule Poirot.'

'Did I not tell you that I was, like you, a very puzzled man? But at least we can face our problem. We can arrange such facts as we have with order and method.'

'Pray continue, Monsieur,' said Dr Constantine.

Poirot cleared his throat and straightened a piece of blotting-paper.

'Let us review the case as it stands at this moment. First, there are certain indisputable facts. This man Ratchett, or Cassetti, was stabbed in twelve places and died last night. That is fact one.'

'I grant it to you – I grant it, *mon vieux*,' said M. Bouc with a gesture of irony.

Hercule Poirot was not at all put out. He continued calmly.

'I will pass over for the moment certain rather peculiar appearances which Dr Constantine and I have already discussed together. I will come to them presently. The next fact of importance, to my mind, is the *time* of the crime.'

'That, again, is one of the few things we do know,' said M. Bouc. 'The crime was committed at a quarter-past one this morning. Everything goes to show that that was so.'

'Not *everything*. You exaggerate. There is, certainly, a fair amount of evidence to support that view.'

'I am glad you admit that at least.'

Poirot went on calmly, unperturbed by the interruption.

'We have before us three possibilities:

'One: That the crime was committed, as you say, at a quarter-past one. This is supported by the evidence of the German woman, Hildegarde Schmidt. It agrees with the evidence of Dr Constantine.

'Possibility two: The crime was committed later and the evidence of the watch was deliberately faked.

'Possibility three: The crime was committed earlier and the evidence faked for the same reason as above.

'Now, if we accept possibility one as the most likely to have occurred and the one supported by most evidence, we must also accept certain facts arising from it. To begin with, if the crime was committed at a quarter-past one, the murderer cannot have left the train, and the question arises: Where is he? And *who* is he?

'To begin with, let us examine the evidence carefully. We first hear of the existence of this man – the small dark man with a womanish voice – from the man Hardman. He says that Ratchett told him of this person and employed him to watch out for the man. There is no *evidence* to support this – we have only Hardman's word for it. Let us next examine the question: Is Hardman the person he pretends to be – an operative of a New York Detective Agency?

'What to my mind is so interesting in this case is that we have none of the facilities afforded to the police. We cannot investigate the bona fides of any of these people. We have to rely solely on deduction. That, to me, makes the matter very much more interesting. There is no routine work. It is a matter of the intellect. I ask myself, "Can we accept Hardman's account of himself?" I make my decision and I answer, "Yes." I am of the opinion that we *can* accept Hardman's account of himself.'

'You rely on the intuition – what the Americans call the hunch?' said Dr Constantine.

'Not at all. I regard the probabilities. Hardman is travelling with a false passport – that will at once make him an object of suspicion. The first thing that the police will do when they do arrive upon the scene is to detain Hardman and cable as to whether his account of himself is true. In the case of many of the passengers, to establish their bona fides will be difficult; in most cases it will probably not be attempted, especially since there seems nothing in the way of suspicion attaching to them. But in Hardman's case it is simple. Either he is the person he represents himself to be or he is not. Therefore I say that all will prove to be in order.'

'You acquit him of suspicion?'

'Not at all. You misunderstand me. For all I know, any American detective might have his own private reasons for wishing to murder Ratchett. No, what I am saying is that I think we *can* accept Hardman's own account of *himself*. This story, then, that he tells of Ratchett's seeking him out and employing him, is not unlikely and is most probably, though not of course certainly, true. If we are going to accept it as true, we must see if there is any confirmation of it. We find it in rather an unlikely place – in the evidence of Hildegarde Schmidt. Her description of the man she saw in Wagon Lit uniform tallies exactly. Is there any further confirmation of these two stories? There is. There is the button found in her compartment by

Mrs Hubbard. And there is also another corroborating statement which you may not have noticed.'

'What is that?'

'The fact that both Colonel Arbuthnot and Hector MacQueen mention that the conductor passed their carriage. They attached no importance to the fact, but Messieurs, *Pierre Michel has declared that he did not leave his seat except on certain specified occasions*, none of which would take him down to the far end of the coach past the compartment in which Arbuthnot and MacQueen were sitting.

'Therefore this story, the story of a small dark man with a womanish voice dressed in Wagon Lit uniform, rests on the testimony – direct or indirect – of four witnesses.'

'One small point,' said Dr Constantine. 'If Hildegarde Schmidt's story is true, how is it that the real conductor did not mention having seen her when he came to answer Mrs Hubbard's bell?'

'That is explained, I think. When he arrived to answer Mrs Hubbard, the maid was in with her mistress. When she finally returned to her own compartment, the conductor was in with Mrs Hubbard.'

M. Bouc had been waiting with difficulty until they had finished.

'Yes, yes, my friend,' he said impatiently to Poirot. 'But whilst I admire your caution, your method of advancing a step at a time, I submit that you have not yet touched the point at issue. We are all agreed that this person exists. The point is – *where did he go?*'

Poirot shook his head reprovingly.

'You are in error. You are inclined to put the cart before the horse. Before I ask myself, *"Where did this man vanish to?"* I ask myself, *"Did such a man really exist?"* Because, you see, if the man were an invention – a fabrication – how much easier to make him disappear! So I try to establish first that there really *is* such a flesh and blood person.'

'And having arrived at the fact that there is – *eh bien* – where is he now?'

'There are only two answers to that, *mon cher.* Either he is still hidden on the train in a place of such extraordinary ingenuity that we cannot even think of it, or else he is, as one might say, *two persons.* That is, he is both himself – the man feared by M. Ratchett – and a passenger on the train so well disguised that M. Ratchett did not recognize him.'

'It is an idea, that,' said M. Bouc, his face lighting up. Then it clouded over again. 'But there is one objection –'

Poirot took the words out of his mouth.

'The height of the man. It is that you would say? With the exception of M. Ratchett's valet, all the passengers are big men – the Italian, Colonel Arbuthnot,

Hector MacQueen, Count Andrenyi. Well, that leaves us the valet – not a very likely supposition. But there is another possibility. Remember the "womanish" voice. That gives us a choice of alternatives. The man may be disguised as a woman, or, alternatively, he may actually *be* a woman. A tall woman dressed in man's clothes would look small.'

'But surely Ratchett would have known –'

'Perhaps he *did* know. Perhaps, already this woman had attempted his life wearing men's clothes the better to accomplish her purpose. Ratchett may have guessed that she would use the same trick again, so he tells Hardman to look for a man. But he mentions, however, a womanish voice.'

'It is a possibility,' said M. Bouc. 'But –'

'Listen, my friend, I think that I should now tell you of certain inconsistencies noticed by Dr Constantine.'

He retailed at length the conclusions that he and the doctor had arrived at together from the nature of the dead man's wounds. M. Bouc groaned and held his head again.

'I know,' said Poirot sympathetically. 'I know exactly how you feel. The head spins, does it not?'

'The whole thing is a fantasy,' cried M. Bouc.

'Exactly. It is absurd – improbable – it cannot be. So I myself have said. And yet, my friend, *there it is*! One cannot escape from the facts.'

'It is madness!'

'Is it not? It is so mad, my friend, that sometimes I am haunted by the sensation that really it must be very simple . . .

'But that is only one of my "little ideas." . . .'

'Two murderers,' groaned M. Bouc. 'And on the Orient Express.'

The thought almost made him weep.

'And now let us make the fantasy more fantastic,' said Poirot cheerfully. 'Last night on the train there are two mysterious strangers. There is the Wagon Lit attendant answering to the description given us by M. Hardman, and seen by Hildegarde Schmidt, Colonel Arbuthnot and M. MacQueen. There is also a woman in a red kimono – a tall, slim woman – seen by Pierre Michel, by Miss Debenham, by M. MacQueen and by myself – and smelt, I may say, by Colonel Arbuthnot! Who was she? No one on the train admits to having a scarlet kimono. She, too, has vanished. Was she one and the same with the spurious Wagon Lit attendant? Or was she some quite distinct personality? Where are they, these two? And, incidentally, where is the Wagon Lit uniform and the scarlet kimono?'

'Ah! that is something definite.' M. Bouc sprang up eagerly. 'We must search all the passengers' luggage. Yes, that will be something.'

Poirot rose also.

'I will make a prophecy,' he said.

'You know where they are?'

'I have a little idea.'

'Where, then?'

'You will find the scarlet kimono in the baggage of one of the men and you will find the uniform of the Wagon Lit conductor in the baggage of Hildegarde Schmidt.'

'Hildegarde Schmidt? You think –'

'Not what you are thinking. I will put it like this. If Hildegarde Schmidt is guilty, the uniform *might* be found in her baggage – but if she is innocent it *certainly* will be.'

'But how –' began M. Bouc and stopped.

'What is this noise that approaches?' he cried. 'It resembles a locomotive in motion.'

The noise drew nearer. It consisted of shrill cries and protests in a woman's voice. The door at the end of the dining-car flew open. Mrs Hubbard burst in.

'It's too horrible,' she cried. 'It's just too horrible. In my sponge-bag. My sponge-bag. A great knife – all over blood.'

And, suddenly toppling forward, she fainted heavily on M. Bouc's shoulder.

Chapter 14

The Evidence of the Weapon

With more vigour than chivalry, M. Bouc deposited the
fainting lady with her head on the table. Dr Constantine
yelled for one of the restaurant attendants, who came
at a run.

'Keep her head so,' said the doctor. 'If she revives
give her a little cognac. You understand?'

Then he hurried off after the other two. His interest
lay wholly in the crime – swooning middle-aged ladies
did not interest him at all.

It is possible that Mrs Hubbard revived rather quicker
with these methods than she might otherwise have
done. A few minutes later she was sitting up, sipping
cognac from a glass proffered by the attendant, and
talking once more.

'I just can't say how terrible it was. I don't suppose
anybody on this train can understand my feelings. I've
always been vurry, vurry sensitive ever since a child.

The mere sight of blood – ugh – why even now I come over queer when I think about it.'

The attendant proffered the glass again.

'*Encore un peu, Madame.*'

'D'you think I'd better? I'm a lifelong teetotaller. I just never touch spirits or wine at any time. All my family are abstainers. Still perhaps as this is only medical –'

She sipped once more.

In the meantime Poirot and M. Bouc, closely followed by Dr Constantine, had hurried out of the restaurant-car and along the corridor of the Stamboul coach towards Mrs Hubbard's compartment.

Every traveller on the train seemed to be congregated outside the door. The conductor, a harrassed look on his face, was keeping them back.

'*Mais il n'y a rien à voir,*' he said, and repeated the sentiment in several other languages.

'Let me pass, if you please,' said M. Bouc.

Squeezing his rotundity past the obstructing passengers, he entered the compartment, Poirot close behind him.

'I am glad you have come Monsieur,' said the conductor with a sigh of relief. 'Everyone has been trying to enter. The American lady – such screams as she gave – *ma foi*! I thought she too had been murdered! I came at a run and there she was screaming like a mad woman, and she cried out that she must fetch you and she departed, screeching at the top of her voice and telling everybody whose carriage she passed what had occurred.'

He added, with a gesture of the hand:

'*It* is in there, Monsieur. I have not touched it.'

Hanging on the handle of the door that gave access to the next compartment was a large-size checked rubber sponge-bag. Below it on the floor, just where it had fallen from Mrs Hubbard's hand, was a straight-bladed dagger – a cheap affair, sham Oriental, with an embossed hilt and a tapering blade. The blade was stained with patches of what looked like rust.

Poirot picked it up delicately.

'Yes,' he murmured. 'There is no mistake. Here is our missing weapon all right – eh, docteur?'

The doctor examined it.

'You need not be so careful,' said Poirot. 'There will be no fingerprints on it save those of Mrs Hubbard.'

Constantine's examination did not take long.

'It is the weapon all right,' he said. 'It would account for any of the wounds.'

'I implore you, my friend, do not say that.'

The doctor looked astonished.

'Already we are heavily overburdened by coincidence. Two people decide to stab M. Ratchett last night. It is too much of a good thing that each of them should select an identical weapon.'

'As to that, the coincidence is not, perhaps, so great as it seems,' said the doctor. 'Thousands of these sham Eastern daggers are made and shipped to the bazaars of Constantinople.'

'You console me a little, but only a little,' said Poirot. He looked thoughtfully at the door in front of him, then, lifting off the sponge-bag, he tried the handle. The door did not budge. About a foot above the handle was the door bolt, Poirot drew it back and tried again, but still the door remained fast.

'We locked it from the other side, you remember,' said the doctor.

'That is true,' said Poirot absently. He seemed to be thinking about something else. His brow was furrowed as though in perplexity.

'It agrees, does it not?' said M. Bouc. 'The man passes through this carriage. As he shuts the communicating door behind him he feels the sponge-bag. A thought comes to him and he quickly slips the bloodstained knife inside. Then, all unwitting that he has awakened Mrs Hubbard, he slips out through the other door into the corridor.'

'As you say,' murmured Poirot. 'That is how it must have happened.'

But the puzzled look did not leave his face.

'But what is it?' demanded M. Bouc. 'There is

something, is there not, that does not satisfy you?'

Poirot darted a quick look at him.

'The same point does not strike you? No, evidently not. Well, it is a small matter.'

The conductor looked into the carriage.

'The American lady is coming back.'

Dr Constantine looked rather guilty. He had, he felt, treated Mrs Hubbard rather cavalierly. But she had no reproaches for him. Her energies were concentrated on another matter.

'I'm just going to say one thing right out,' she said breathlessly as she arrived in the doorway. 'I'm not going on any longer in this compartment! Why, I wouldn't sleep in it tonight if you paid me a million dollars.'

'But, Madame –'

'I know what you are going to say, and I'm telling you right now that I won't do any such thing! Why, I'd rather sit up all night in the corridor.'

She began to cry.

'Oh! if my daughter could only know – if she could see me now, why –'

Poirot interrupted firmly.

'You misunderstand, Madame. Your demand is most reasonable. Your baggage shall be changed at once to another compartment.'

Mrs Hubbard lowered her handkerchief.

'Is that so? Oh, I feel better right away. But surely it's all full up, unless one of the gentlemen –'

M. Bouc spoke.

'Your baggage, Madame, shall be moved out of this coach altogether. You shall have a compartment in the next coach which was put on at Belgrade.'

'Why, that's splendid. I'm not an out of the way nervous woman, but to sleep in that compartment next door to a dead man –' She shivered. 'It would drive me plumb crazy.'

'Michel,' called M. Bouc. 'Move this baggage into a vacant compartment in the Athens-Paris coach.'

'Yes, Monsieur – the same one as this – the No. 3?'

'No,' said Poirot before his friend could reply. 'I think it would be better for Madame to have a different number altogether. The No. 12, for instance.'

'*Bien*, Monsieur.'

The conductor seized the luggage. Mrs Hubbard turned gratefully to Poirot.

'That's vurry kind and delicate of you. I appreciate it, I assure you.'

'Do not mention it, Madame. We will come with you and see you comfortably installed.'

Mrs Hubbard was escorted by the three men to her new home. She looked round her happily.

'This is fine.'

'It suits you, Madame? It is, you see, exactly like the compartment you have left.'

'That's so – only it faces the other way. But that doesn't matter, for these trains go first one way and then the other. I said to my daughter, "I want a carriage facing the engine," and she said, "Why, Momma, that'll be no good to you, for if you go to sleep one way, when you wake up the train's going the other." And it was quite true what she said. Why, last evening we went into Belgrade one way and out the other.'

'At any rate, Madame, you are quite happy and contented now?'

'Well, no, I wouldn't say that. Here we are stuck in a snowdrift and nobody doing anything about it, and my boat sailing the day after tomorrow.'

'Madame,' said M. Bouc, 'we are all in the same case – every one of us.'

'Well, that's true,' admitted Mrs Hubbard. 'But nobody else has had a murderer walking right through their compartment in the middle of the night.'

'What still puzzles me, Madame,' said Poirot, 'is how the man got into your compartment if the communicating door was bolted as you say. You are sure that it *was* bolted?'

'Why, the Swedish lady tried it before my eyes.'

'Let us just reconstruct that little scene. You were

lying in your bunk – so – and you could not see for yourself, you say?'

'No, because of the sponge-bag. Oh, my, I shall have to get a new sponge-bag. It makes me feel sick in my stomach to look at this one.'

Poirot picked up the sponge-bag and hung it on the handle of the communicating door into the next carriage.

'*Précisément* – I see,' he said. 'The bolt is just underneath the handle – the sponge-bag masks it. You could not see from where you were lying whether the bolt were turned or not.'

'Why, that's just what I've been telling you!'

'And the Swedish lady, Miss Ohlsson, stood so, between you and the door. She tried it and told you it was bolted.'

'That's so.'

'All the same, Madame, she may have made an error. You see what I mean.' Poirot seemed anxious to explain. 'The bolt is just a projection of metal – so. Turned to the right the door is locked, left straight, it is not. Possibly she merely tried the door, and as it was locked on the other side she may have assumed that it was locked on your side.'

'Well I guess that would be rather stupid of her.'

'Madame, the most kind, the most amiable are not always the cleverest.'

'That's so, of course.'

'By the way, Madame, did you travel out to Smyrna this way?'

'No. I sailed right to Stamboul, and a friend of my daughter's – Mr Johnson (a perfectly lovely man; I'd like to have you know him) – met me and showed me all round Stamboul, which I found a very disappointing city – all tumbling down. And as for those mosques and putting on those great shuffling things over your shoes – where was I?'

'You were saying that Mr Johnson met you.'

'That's so, and he saw me on board a French Messagerie boat for Smyrna, and my daughter's husband was waiting right on the quay. What he'll say when he hears about all this! My daughter said this would be just the safest, easiest way imaginable. "You just sit in your carriage," she said, "and you get right to Parrus and there the American Express will meet you." And, oh dear, what am I to do about cancelling my steamship passage? I ought to let them know. I can't possibly make it now. This is just too terrible –'

Mrs Hubbard showed signs of tears once more.

Poirot, who had been fidgeting slightly, seized his opportunity.

'You have had a shock, Madame. The restaurant attendant shall be instructed to bring you along some tea and some biscuits.'

'I don't know that I'm so set on tea,' said Mrs Hubbard tearfully. 'That's more an English habit.'

'Coffee, then, Madame. You need some stimulant.'

'That cognac's made my head feel mighty funny. I think I would like some coffee.'

'Excellent. You must revive your forces.'

'My, what a funny expression.'

'But first, Madame, a little matter of routine. You permit that I make a search of your baggage?'

'Whatever for?'

'We are about to commence a search of all the passengers' luggage. I do not want to remind you of an unpleasant experience, but your sponge-bag – remember.'

'Mercy! Perhaps you'd better! I just couldn't bear to get any more surprises of that kind.'

The examination was quickly over. Mrs Hubbard was travelling with the minimum of luggage – a hat box, a cheap suitcase, and a well-burdened travelling bag. The contents of all three were simple and straightforward, and the examination would not have taken more than a couple of minutes had not Mrs Hubbard delayed matters by insisting on due attention being paid to photographs of 'My daughter' and two rather ugly children – 'My daughter's children. Aren't they cunning?'

Chapter 15

The Evidence of the
Passengers' Luggage

Having delivered himself of various polite insincerities, and having told Mrs Hubbard that he would order coffee to be brought to her, Poirot was able to take his leave accompanied by his two friends.

'Well, we have made a start and drawn a blank,' observed M. Bouc. 'Whom shall we tackle next?'

'It would be simplest, I think, just to proceed along the train carriage by carriage. That means that we start with No. 16 – the amiable M. Hardman.'

Mr Hardman, who was smoking a cigar, welcomed them affably.

'Come right in, gentlemen – that is, if it's humanly possible. It's just a mite cramped in here for a party.'

M. Bouc explained the object of their visit, and the big detective nodded comprehendingly.

'That's O.K. To tell the truth, I've been wondering you didn't get down to it sooner. Here are my keys, gentlemen and if you like to search my pockets too, why, you're welcome. Shall I reach the grips down for you?'

'The conductor will do that. Michel!'

The contents of Mr Hardman's two 'grips' were soon examined and passed. They contained perhaps an undue proportion of spirituous liquor. Mr Hardman winked.

'It's not often they search your grips at the frontiers – not if you fix the conductor. I handed out a wad of Turkish notes right away, and there's been no trouble so far.'

'And at Paris?'

Mr Hardman winked again.

'By the time I get to Paris,' he said, 'what's left over of this little lot will go into a bottle labelled hairwash.'

'You are not a believer in Prohibition, Monsieur Hardman,' said M. Bouc with a smile.

'Well,' said Hardman. 'I can't say Prohibition has ever worried me any.'

'Ah!' said M. Bouc. 'The speakeasy.' He pronounced the word with care, savouring it.

'Your American terms are so quaint, so expressive,' he said.

'Me, I would much like to go to America,' said Poirot.

'You'd learn a few go-ahead methods over there,' said Hardman. 'Europe wants waking up. She's half asleep.'

'It is true that America is the country of progress,' agreed Poirot. 'There is much that I admire about Americans. Only – I am perhaps old-fashioned – but me, I find the American woman less charming than my own countrywomen. The French or Belgian girl, coquettish, charming – I think there is no one to touch her.'

Hardman turned away to peer out at the snow for a minute.

'Perhaps you're right, M. Poirot,' he said. 'But I guess every nation likes its own girls best.'

He blinked as though the snow hurt his eyes.

'Kind of dazzling, isn't it?' he remarked. 'Say, gentlemen, this business is getting on my nerves. Murder and the snow and all, and nothing *doing*. Just hanging about and killing time. I'd like to get busy after someone or something.'

'The true Western spirit of hustle,' said Poirot with a smile.

The conductor replaced the bags and they moved on to the next compartment. Colonel Arbuthnot was sitting in a corner smoking a pipe and reading a magazine.

Poirot explained their errand. The Colonel made

no demur. He had two heavy leather suitcases.

'The rest of my kit has gone by long sea,' he explained.

Like most Army men, the Colonel was a neat packer. The examination of his baggage took only a few minutes. Poirot noted a packet of pipe-cleaners.

'You always use the same kind?' he asked.

'Usually. If I can get 'em.'

'Ah!' Poirot nodded.

These pipe-cleaners were identical with the one he had found on the floor of the dead man's compartment.

Dr Constantine remarked as much when they were out in the corridor again.

'*Tout de même,*' murmured Poirot, 'I can hardly believe it. It is not *dans son caractère,* and when you have said that you have said everything.'

The door of the next compartment was closed. It was that occupied by Princess Dragomiroff. They knocked on the door and the Princess's deep voice called, '*Entrez.*'

M. Bouc was spokesman. He was very deferential and polite as he explained their errand.

The Princess listened to him in silence, her small toad-like face quite impassive.

'If it is necessary, Messieurs,' she said quietly when

he had finished, 'that is all there is to it. My maid has the keys. She will attend to it with you.'

'Does your maid always carry your keys, Madame?' asked Poirot.

'Certainly, Monsieur.'

'And if during the night at one of the frontiers the Customs officials should require a piece of luggage to be opened?'

The old lady shrugged her shoulders.

'It is very unlikely. But in such a case this conductor would fetch her.'

'You trust her, then, implicitly, Madame?'

'I have told you so already,' said the Princess quietly. 'I do not employ people whom I do not trust.'

'Yes,' said Poirot thoughtfully. 'Trust is indeed something in these days. It is, perhaps, better to have a homely woman whom one can trust than a more *chic* maid – for example, some smart Parisienne.'

He saw the dark intelligent eyes come slowly round and fasten themselves upon his face.

'What exactly are you implying, M. Poirot?'

'Nothing, Madame. I? Nothing.'

'But yes. You think, do you not, that I should have a smart Frenchwoman to attend to my toilet?'

'It would be, perhaps, more usual, Madame.'

She shook her head.

'Schmidt is devoted to me.' Her voice dwelt lingeringly

on the words. 'Devotion – *c'est impayable.*'

The German woman had arrived with the keys. The Princess spoke to her in her own language, telling her to open the valises and help the gentlemen in their search. She herself remained in the corridor looking out at the snow and Poirot remained with her, leaving M. Bouc to the task of searching the luggage.

She regarded him with a grim smile.

'Well, Monsieur, do you not wish to see what my valises contain?'

He shook his head.

'Madame, it is a formality, that is all.'

'Are you so sure?'

'In your case, yes.'

'And yet I knew and loved Sonia Armstrong. What do you think, then? That I would not soil my hands with killing such *canaille* as that man Cassetti? Well, perhaps you are right.'

She was silent a minute or two, then she said:

'With such a man as that, do you know what I should have liked to have done? I should have liked to call to my servants: "Flog this man to death and fling him out on the rubbish heap." That is the way things were done when I was young. Monsieur.'

Still he did not speak, just listened attentively.

She looked at him with a sudden impetuosity.

'You do not say anything, M. Poirot. What is it that you are thinking, I wonder?'

He looked at her with a very direct glance.

'I think, Madame, that your strength is in your will – not in your arm.'

She glanced down at her thin, black-clad arms ending in those claw-like yellow hands with the rings on the fingers.

'It is true,' she said. 'I have no strength in these – none. I do not know if I am sorry or glad.'

Then she turned abruptly back towards her carriage, where the maid was busily packing up the cases.

The Princess cut short M. Bouc's apologies.

'There is not need for you to apologize, Monsieur,' she said. 'A murder has been committed. Certain actions have to be performed. That is all there is to it.'

'*Vous êtes bien amiable, Madame.*'

She inclined her head slightly as they departed.

The doors of the next two carriages were shut. M. Bouc paused and scratched his head.

'Diable!' he said. 'This may be awkward. These are diplomatic passports. Their baggage is exempt.'

'From Customs examination, yes. But a murder is different.'

'I know. All the same – we do not want to have complications –'

'Do not distress yourself, my friend. The Count and Countess will be reasonable. See how amiable Princess Dragomiroff was about it.'

'She is truly *grande dame*. These two are also of the same position, but the Count impressed me as a man of somewhat truculent disposition. He was not pleased when you insisted on questioning his wife. And this will annoy him still further. Suppose – eh – we omit them. After all, they can have nothing to do with the matter. Why should I stir up needless trouble for myself.'

'I do not agree with you,' said Poirot. 'I feel sure that Count Andrenyi will be reasonable. At any rate, let us make the attempt.'

And, before M. Bouc could reply, he rapped sharply on the door of No. 13.

A voice from within cried, '*Entrez*.'

The Count was sitting in the corner near the door reading a newspaper. The Countess was curled up in the opposite corner near the window. There was a pillow behind her head, and she seemed to have been asleep.

'Pardon, Monsieur le Comte,' began Poirot. 'Pray forgive this intrusion. It is that we are making a search of all the baggage on the train. In most cases a mere formality. But it has to be done. M. Bouc suggests that, as you have a diplomatic passport, you might reasonably claim to be exempt from such a search.'

The Count considered for a moment.

'Thank you,' he said. 'But I do not think that I care for an exception to be made in my case. I should prefer that our baggage should be examined like that of the other passengers.'

He turned to his wife.

'You do not object, I hope, Elena?'

'Not at all,' said the Countess without hesitation.

A rapid and somewhat perfunctory search followed. Poirot seemed to be trying to mask an embarrassment in making various small pointless remarks, such as:

'Here is a label all wet on your suitcase, Madame,' as he lifted down a blue morocco case with initials on it and a coronet.

The Countess did not reply to this observation. She seemed, indeed, rather bored by the whole proceeding, remaining curled up in her corner, staring dreamily out through the window whilst the men searched her luggage in the compartment next door.

Poirot finished his search by opening the little cupboard above the wash-basin and taking a rapid glance at its contents – a sponge, face cream, powder and a small bottle labelled trional.

Then, with polite remarks on either side, the search party withdrew.

Mrs Hubbard's compartment, that of the dead man, and Poirot's own came next.

They now came to the second-class carriages. The first one, Nos. 10, 11, was occupied by Mary Debenham, who was reading a book, and Greta Ohlsson, who was fast asleep but woke with a start at their entrance.

Poirot repeated his formula. The Swedish lady seemed agitated, Mary Debenham calmly indifferent.

Poirot addressed himself to the Swedish lady.

'If you permit, Mademoiselle, we will examine your baggage first, and then perhaps you would be so good as to see how the American lady is getting on. We have moved her into one of the carriages in the next coach, but she is still very upset as the result of her discovery. I have ordered coffee to be sent to her, but I think she is of those to whom someone to talk to is a necessity of the first water.'

The good lady was instantly sympathetic. She would go immediately. It must have been indeed a terrible shock to the nerves, and already the poor lady was upset by the journey and leaving her daugher. Ah, yes, certainly she would go at once – her case was not locked – and she would take with her some sal ammoniac.

She bustled off. Her possessions were soon examined. They were meagre in the extreme. She had evidently not noticed the missing wires from the hat box.

Miss Debenham had put her book down. She was watching Poirot. When he asked her, she handed over her keys. Then, as he lifted down a case and opened it, she said:

'Why did you send her away, M. Poirot?'

'I, Mademoiselle? Why, to minister to the American lady.'

'An excellent pretext – but a pretext all the same.'

'I don't understand you, Mademoiselle.'

'I think you understand me very well.'

She smiled.

'You wanted to get me alone. Wasn't that it?'

'You are putting words into my mouth, Mademoiselle.'

'And ideas into your head? No, I don't think so. The ideas are already there. That is right, isn't it?'

'Mademoiselle, we have a proverb –'

'*Que s'excuse s'accuse*; is that what you were going to say? You must give me the credit for a certain amount of observation and common sense. For some reason or other you have got it into your head that I know something about this sordid business – this murder of a man I never saw before.'

'You are imagining things, Mademoiselle.'

'No, I am not imagining things at all. But it seems to me that a lot of time is wasted by not speaking the truth – by beating about the bush instead of coming straight out with things.'

'And you do not like the waste of time. No, you like to come straight to the point. You like the direct method. *Eh bien*, I will give it to you, the direct method. I will ask you the meaning of certain words that I overheard on the journey from Syria. I had got out of the train to do what the English call "stretch the legs" at the station of Konya. Your voice and the Colonel's, Mademoiselle, they came to me out of the night. You said to him, "*Not now. Not now. When it's all over. When it's behind us.*" What did you mean by those words. Mademoiselle?'

She said very quietly:

'Do you think I meant – murder?'

'It is I who am asking you, Mademoiselle.'

She sighed – was lost a minute in thought. Then, as though rousing herself, she said:

'Those words had a meaning, Monsieur, but not one that I can tell you. I can only give you my solemn word of honour that I had never set eyes on this man Ratchett in my life until I saw him on this train.'

'And – you refuse to explain those words?'

'Yes – if you like to put it that way – I refuse. They had to do with – with a task I had undertaken.'

'A task that is now ended?'

'What do you mean?'

'It is ended, is it not?'

'Why should you think so?'

'Listen, Mademoiselle, I will recall to you another incident. There was a delay to the train on the day we were to reach Stamboul. You were very agitated, Mademoiselle. You, so calm, so self-controlled. You lost that calm.'

'I did not want to miss my connection.'

'So you said. But, Mademoiselle, the Orient Express leaves Stamboul every day of the week. Even if you had missed the connection it would only have been a matter of twenty-four hours' delay.'

Miss Debenham for the first time showed signs of losing her temper.

'You do not seem to realize that one may have friends awaiting one's arrival in London, and that a day's delay upsets arrangements and causes a lot of annoyance.'

'Ah, it is like that? There are friends awaiting your arrival? You do not want to cause them inconvenience?'

'Naturally.'

'And yet – it is curious –'

'What is curious?'

'On this train – again we have a delay. And this time a more serious delay, since there is no possibility of sending a telegram to your friends or of getting them on the long – the long –'

'The long distance? The telephone, you mean.'

'Ah, yes, the portmanteau call, as you say in England.'

Mary Debenham smiled a little in spite of herself.

'Trunk call,' she corrected. 'Yes, as you say, it is extremely annoying not to be able to get any word through, either by telephone or telegraph.'

'And yet, mademoiselle, *this* time your manner is quite different. You no longer betray the impatience. You are calm and philosophical.'

Mary Debenham flushed and bit her lip. She no longer felt inclined to smile.

'You do not answer, Mademoiselle?'

'I am sorry. I did not know that there was anything to answer.'

'The explanation of your change of attitude, Mademoiselle.'

'Don't you think that you are making rather a fuss about nothing, M. Poirot?'

Poirot spread out his hands in an apologetic gesture.

'It is perhaps a fault with us detectives. We expect the behaviour to be always consistent. We do not allow for changes of mood.'

Mary Debenham made no reply.

'You know Colonel Arbuthnot well, Mademoiselle?'

He fancied that she was relieved by the change of subject.

'I met him for the first time on this journey.'

'Have you any reason to suspect that he may have known this man Ratchett?'

She shook her head decisively.

'I am quite sure he didn't.'

'Why are you sure?'

'By the way he spoke.'

'And yet, Mademoiselle, we found a pipe-cleaner on the floor of the dead man's compartment. And Colonel Arbuthnot is the only man on the train who smokes a pipe?'

He watched her narrowly, but she displayed neither surprise nor emotion, merely said:

'Nonsense. It's absurd. Colonel Arbuthnot is the last man in the world to be mixed up in a crime – especially a theatrical kind of crime like this.'

It was so much what Poirot himself thought that he found himself on the point of agreeing with her. He said instead:

'I must remind you that you do not know him very well, Mademoiselle.'

She shrugged her shoulders.

'I know the type well enough.'

He said very gently:

'You still refuse to tell me the meaning of those words – "When it's behind us"?'

She said coldly:

'I have nothing more to say.'

'It does not matter,' said Hercule Poirot. 'I shall find out.'

He bowed and left the compartment, closing the door after him.

'Was that wise, my friend?' asked M. Bouc. 'You have put her on her guard – and through her you have put the Colonel on his guard also.'

'*Mon ami*, if you wish to catch a rabbit you put a ferret into the hole, and if the rabbit is there he runs. That is all I have done.'

They entered the compartment of Hildegarde Schmidt.

The woman was standing in readiness, her face respectful but unemotional.

Poirot took a quick glance through the contents of the small case on the seat. Then he motioned to the attendant to get down the bigger suitcase from the rack.

'The keys?' he said.

'It is not locked, Monsieur.'

Poirot undid the hasps and lifted the lid.

'Aha!' he said, and turning to M. Bouc, 'You remember what I said? Look here a little moment!'

On the top of the suitcase was a hastily rolled up brown Wagon Lit uniform.

The stolidity of the German woman underwent a sudden change.

'Ach!' she cried. 'That is not mine. I did not put it there. I have never looked in that case since we left Stamboul. Indeed, indeed, it is true.'

She looked from one to another pleadingly.

Poirot took her gently by the arm and soothed her.

'No, no all is well. We believe you. Do not be agitated. I am as sure you did not hide the uniform there as I am sure that you are a good cook. See. You are a good cook, are you not?'

Bewildered, the woman smiled in spite of herself.

'Yes, indeed, all my ladies have said so. I —'

She stopped, her mouth open, looking frightened again.

'No, no,' said Poirot. 'I assure you all is well. See, I will tell you how this happened. This man, the man you saw in Wagon Lit uniform, comes out of the dead man's compartment. He collides with you. That is bad luck for him. He has hoped that no one will see him. What to do next? He must get rid of his uniform. It is now not a safeguard, but a danger.'

His glance went to M. Bouc and Dr Constantine, who were listening attentively.

'There is the snow, you see. The snow which confuses all his plans. Where can he hide these clothes? All the compartments are full. No, he passes one where the door is open and shows it to be unoccupied. It must be the one belonging to the woman with whom he has just collided. He slips in, removes the uniform and jams it hurriedly into a suitcase on the rack. It may be some time before it is discovered.'

'And then?' said M. Bouc.

'That we must discuss,' said Poirot with a warning glance.

He held up the tunic. A button, the third down, was missing. Poirot slipped his hand into the pocket and took out a conductor's pass key, used to unlock the doors of the compartments.

'Here is the explanation of how our man was able to pass through locked doors,' said M. Bouc. 'Your questions to Mrs Hubbard were unnecessary. Locked or not locked, the man could easily get through the communicating door. After all, if a Wagon Lit uniform, why not a Wagon Lit key?'

'Why not, indeed,' said Poirot.

'We might have known it, really. You remember Michel said that the door into the corridor of Mrs Hubbard's compartment was locked when he came in answer to her bell.'

'That is so, Monsieur,' said the conductor. 'That

is why I thought the lady must have been dreaming.'

'But now it is easy,' continued M. Bouc. 'Doubtless he meant to relock the communicating door also, but perhaps he heard some movement from the bed and it startled him.'

'We have now,' said Poirot, 'only to find the scarlet kimono.'

'True. And these last two compartments are occupied by men.'

'We will search all the same.'

'Oh! assuredly. Besides, I remember what you said.'

Hector MacQueen acquiesced willingly in the search.

'I'd just as soon you did,' he said with a rueful smile. 'I feel I'm just definitely the most suspicious character on the train. You've only got to find a will in which the old man left me all his money, and that'll just about fix things.'

M. Bouc bent a suspicious glance upon him.

'That's just my fun,' said MacQueen hastily. 'He'd never have left me a cent, really. I was just useful to him – languages and so on. You're apt to be done down, you know, if you don't speak anything but good American. I'm no linguist myself, but I know what I call shopping and hotel snappy bits in French and German and Italian.'

His voice was a little louder than usual. It was as

though he was slightly uneasy at the search in spite of his willingness.

Poirot emerged.

'Nothing,' he said. 'Not even a compromising bequest!'

MacQueen sighed.

'Well, that's a load off my mind,' he said humorously.

They moved on to the last compartment. The examination of the luggage of the big Italian and of the valet yielded no result.

The three men stood at the end of the coach looking at each other.

'What next?' asked M. Bouc.

'We will go back to the dining-car,' said Poirot. 'We know now all that we can know. We have the evidence of the passengers, the evidence of their baggage, the evidence of our eyes. We can expect no further help. It must be our part now to use our brains.'

He felt in his pocket for his cigarette case. It was empty.

'I will join you in a moment,' he said. 'I shall need the cigarettes. This is a very difficult, a very curious affair. Who wore that scarlet kimono? Where is it now? I wish I knew. There is something in this case – some factor – that escapes me! It is difficult because it has been made difficult. But we will discuss it. Pardon me a moment.'

He went hurriedly along the corridor to his own compartment. He had, he knew, a further supply of cigarettes in one of his valises.

He got it down and snapped back the lock.

Then he sat back on his heels and stared.

Neatly folded on the top of the case was a thin scarlet silk kimono embroidered with dragons.

'So,' he murmured. 'It is like that. A defiance. Very well. I take it up.'

Part 3

Hercule Poirot Sits Back and Thinks

Chapter 1

Which of Them?

M. Bouc and Dr Constantine were talking together when Poirot entered the dining-car. M. Bouc was looking depressed.

'*Le voilà*,' said the latter when he saw Poirot.

Then he added as his friend sat down:

'If you solve this case, *mon cher*, I shall indeed believe in miracles!'

'It worries you, this case?'

'Naturally it worries me. I cannot make head or tail of it.'

'I agree,' said the doctor.

He looked at Poirot with interest.

'To be frank,' he said, 'I cannot see what you are going to do next.'

'No?' said Poirot thoughtfully.

He took out his cigarette case and lit one of his tiny cigarettes. His eyes were dreamy.

'That, to me, is the interest of this case,' he said. 'We are cut off from all the normal routes of procedure. Are these people whose evidence we have taken speaking the truth or lying? We have no means of finding out – except such means as we can devise ourselves. It is an exercise, this, of the brain.'

'That is all very fine,' said M. Bouc. 'But what have you to go upon?'

'I told you just now. We have the evidence of the passengers and the evidence of our own eyes.'

'Pretty evidence – that of the passengers! It told us just nothing at all.'

Poirot shook his head.

'I do not agree, my friend. The evidence of the passengers gave us several points of interest.'

'Indeed,' said M. Bouc sceptically. 'I did not observe it.'

'That is because you did not listen.'

'Well, tell me – what did I miss?'

'I will just take one instance – the first evidence we heard – that of the young MacQueen. He uttered, to my mind, one very significant phrase.'

'About the letters?'

'No, not about the letters. As far as I can remember, his words were: *"We travelled about. Mr Ratchett wanted to see the world. He was hampered by knowing no languages. I acted more as a courier than a secretary".*'

He looked from the doctor's face to that of M. Bouc.

'What? You still do not see? That is inexcusable – for you had a second chance again just now when he said, "*You're apt to be done down if you speak nothing but good American.*"'

'You mean –?' M. Bouc still looked puzzled.

'Ah, it is that you want it given to you in words of one syllable. Well, here it is! *M. Ratchett spoke no French*. Yet, when the conductor came in answer to his bell last night, it was a voice speaking in *French* that told him that it was a mistake and that he was not wanted. It was, moreover, a perfectly idiomatic phrase that was used, not one that a man knowing only a few words of French would have selected. "*Ce n'est rien. Je me suis trompé.*"'

'It is true,' cried Constantine excitedly. 'We should have seen that! I remember your laying stress on the words when you repeated them to us. Now I understand your reluctance to rely upon the evidence of the dented watch. Already, at twenty-three minutes to one, Ratchett was dead –'

'And it was his murderer speaking!' finished M. Bouc impressively.

Poirot raised a deprecating hand.

'Let us not go too fast. And do not let us assume more than we actually know. It is safe, I think, to say that at that time, twenty-three minutes to one, *some other person* was in Ratchett's compartment and that that person was either French, or could speak the French language fluently.'

'You are very cautious, *mon vieux*.'

'One should advance only a step at a time. We have no actual *evidence* that Ratchett was dead at that time.'

'There is the cry that awakened you.'

'Yes, that is true.'

'In one way,' said M. Bouc thoughtfully, 'this discovery does not affect things very much. You heard someone moving about next door. That someone was not Ratchett, but the other man. Doubtless he is washing blood from his hands, clearing up after the crime, burning the incriminating letter. Then he waits till all is still, and when he thinks it is safe and the coast is clear he locks and chains Ratchett's door on the inside, unlocks the communicating door through into Mrs Hubbard's compartment and slips out that way. In fact it is exactly as we thought – *with the difference that Ratchett was killed about half an hour earlier*, and the watch put on to a quarter-past one to create an alibi.'

'Not such a famous alibi,' said Poirot. 'The hands of the watch pointed to 1.15 – the exact time when the intruder actually left the scene of the crime.'

'True,' said M. Bouc, a little confused. 'What, then, does the watch convey to you?'

'If the hands were altered – I say *if* – then the time at which they were set *must* have a significance. The natural reaction would be to suspect anyone who had a reliable alibi for the time indicated – in this case 1.15.'

'Yes, Yes,' said the doctor. 'That reasoning is good.'

'We must also pay a little attention to the time the intruder *entered* the compartment. When had he an opportunity of doing so? Unless we are to assume the complicity of the real conductor, there was only one time when he could have done so – during the time the train stopped at Vincovci. After the train left Vincovci the conductor was sitting facing the corridor and whereas any one of the passengers would pay little attention to a Wagon Lit attendant, the *one* person who would notice an imposter would be the real conductor. But during the halt at Vincovci the conductor is out on the platform. The coast is clear.'

'And, by our former reasoning, it *must* be one of the passengers,' said M. Bouc. 'We come back to where we were. Which of them?'

Poirot smiled.

'I have made a list,' he said, 'If you like to see it, it will, perhaps, refresh your memory.'

The doctor and M. Bouc pored over the list together. It was written out neatly in a methodical manner in the order in which the passengers had been interviewed.

Hector MacQueen – American subject. Berth No. 6. Second Class.

Motive: Possibly arising out of association with dead man?

Alibi: From midnight to 2 a.m. (Midnight to 1.30 vouched for by Col. Arbuthnot and 1.15 to 2 vouched for by conductor.)

Evidence Against Him: None.

Suspicious Circumstances: None.

Conductor – Pierre Michel – French subject.

Motive: None.

Alibi: From midnight to 2 a.m. (Seen by H.P. in corridor at same time as voice spoke from Ratchett's compartment at 12.37. From 1 a.m. to 1.16 vouched for by other two conductors.)

Evidence Against Him: None.

Suspicious Circumstances: The Wagon Lit uniform found is a point in his favour since it seems to have been intended to throw suspicion on him.

Edward Masterman – English subject. Berth No. 4. Second Class

Motive: Possibly arising out of connection with deceased, whose valet he was.

Alibi: From midnight to 2 a.m. (Vouched for by Antonio Foscarelli.)

Evidence Against Him or Suspicious Circumstances: None,

except that he is the only man the right height or size to have worn the Wagon Lit uniform. On the other hand, it is unlikely that he speaks French well.

Mrs Hubbard – American subject. Berth No. 3. First Class.

Motive: None.

Alibi: From midnight to 2 a.m. – None.

Evidence Against Her or Suspicious Circumstances: Story of man in her compartment is substantiated by the evidence of Hardman and that of the woman Schmidt.

Greta Ohlsson – Swedish subject. Berth No. 10. Second Class.

Motive: None.

Alibi: From midnight to 2 a.m. (Vouched for by Mary Debenham). Note. – Was last to see Ratchett alive.

Princess Dragomiroff – Naturalized French subject. Berth No. 14. First Class.

Motive: Was intimately acquainted with Armstrong family, and godmother to Sonia Armstrong.

Alibi: From midnight to 2 a.m. (Vouched for by conductor and maid.)

Evidence Against Her or Suspicious Circumstances: None.

Count Andrenyi – Hungarian subject. Diplomatic passport. Berth No. 13. First Class.

Motive: None.

Alibi: Midnight to 2 a.m. (Vouched for by conductor – this does not cover period from 1 to 1.15.)

Countess Andrenyi – As above. Berth No. 12.
Motive: None.
Alibi: Midnight to 2 a.m. Took trional and slept. (Vouched for by husband. Trional bottle in her cupboard.)

Colonel Arbuthnot – British subject. Berth No. 15.
First Class
Motive: None.
Alibi: Midnight to 2 a.m. Talked with MacQueen till 1.30. Went to own compartment and did not leave it. (Substantiated by MacQueen and conductor.)
Evidence Against Him or Suspicious Circumstances: Pipe-cleaner.

Cyrus Hardman – American subject. Berth No. 16.
Second Class
Motive: None known.
Alibi: Midnight to 2 a.m. Did not leave compartment. (Substantiated by MacQueen and conductor.)
Evidence Against Him or Suspicious Circumstances: None.

Antonio Foscarelli – American subject. (Italian birth.)
Berth No. 5. Second Class
Motive: None known.
Alibi: Midnight to 2 a.m. (Vouched for by Edward Masterman.)

Evidence Against Him or Suspicious Circumstances: None, except that weapon used might be said to suit his temperament. (Vide M. Bouc.)

Mary Debenham – British subject. Berth No. 11.
Second Class
   Motive: None.
   Alibi: Midnight to 2 a.m. (Vouched for by Greta Ohlsson.)
   Evidence Against Her or Suspicious Circumstances: and her refusal to explain same.

Hildegarde Schmidt – German subject. Berth No. 8.
Second Class.
   Motive: None.
   Alibi: Midnight to 2 a.m. (Vouched for by conductor and her mistress.) Went to bed. Was aroused by conductor at 12.38 approx. and went to mistress.

Note: The evidence of the passengers is supported by the statement of the conductor that no one entered or left Mr Ratchett's compartment between the hours of midnight to 1 o'clock (when he himself went into the next coach) and from 1.15 to 2 o'clock.

'That document, you understand,' said Poirot, 'is a mere précis of the evidence we heard, arranged that way for convenience.'

With a grimace M. Bouc handed it back.

Agatha Christie

'It is not illuminating,' he said.

'Perhaps you may find this more to your taste,' said Poirot with a slight smile as he handed him a second sheet of paper.

Chapter 2

Ten Questions

On the paper was written:

Things needing explanation.

1. The handkerchief marked with the initial H. Whose is it?
2. The pipe-cleaner. Was it dropped by Colonel Arbuthnot? Or by someone else?
3. Who wore the scarlet kimono?
4. Who was the man or woman masquerading in Wagon Lit uniform?
5. Why do the hands of the watch point to 1.15?
6. Was the murder committed at that time?
7. Was it earlier?
8. Was it later?
9. Can we be sure that Ratchett was stabbed by more than one person?
10. What other explanation of his wounds can there be?

'Well, let us see what we can do,' said M. Bouc, brightening a little at this challenge to his wits. 'The handkerchief to begin with. Let us by all means be orderly and methodical.'

'Assuredly,' said Poirot, nodding his head in a satisfied fashion.

M. Bouc continued somewhat didactically.

'The initial H is connected with three people – Mrs Hubbard, Miss Debenham, whose second name is Hermione, and the maid Hildegarde Schmidt.'

'Ah! And of those three?'

'It is difficult to say. But I *think* I should vote for Miss Debenham. For all one knows, she may be called by her second name and not her first. Also there is already some suspicion attaching to her. That conversation you overheard, *mon cher*, was certainly a little curious, and so is her refusal to explain it.'

'As for me, I plump for the American,' said Dr Constantine. 'It is a very expensive handkerchief that, and Americans, as all the world knows, do not care what they pay.'

'So you both eliminate the maid?' asked Poirot.

'Yes. As she herself said, it is the handkerchief of a member of the upper classes.'

'And the second question – the pipe-cleaner. Did Colonel Arbuthnot drop it, or somebody else?'

'That is more difficult. The English, they do not

stab. You are right there. I incline to the view that someone else dropped the pipe-cleaner – and did so to incriminate the long-legged Englishman.'

'As you said, M. Poirot,' put in the doctor, '*two* clues is too much carelessness. I agree with M. Bouc. The handkerchief was a genuine oversight – hence no one will admit that it is theirs. The pipe-cleaner is a faked clue. In support of that theory, you notice that Colonel Arbuthnot shows no embarrassment and admits freely to smoking a pipe and using that type of cleaner.'

'You reason well,' said Poirot.

'Question No. 3 – who wore the scarlet kimono?' went on M. Bouc. 'As to that I will confess I have not the slightest idea. Have you any views on the subject, Dr Constantine?'

'None.'

'Then we confess ourselves beaten there. The next question has, at any rate, possibilities. Who was the man or woman masquerading in Wagon Lit uniform? Well, one can say with certainty a number of people whom it could *not* be. Hardman, Colonel Arbuthnot, Foscarelli, Count Andrenyi and Hector MacQueen are all too tall. Mrs Hubbard, Hildegarde Schmidt and Greta Ohlsson are too broad. That leaves the valet, Miss Debenham, Princess Dragomiroff and Countess Andrenyi – and none of them sounds likely! Greta

Ohlsson in one case and Antonio Foscarelli in the other both swear that Miss Debenham and the valet never left their compartments, Hildegarde Schmidt swears to the Princess being in hers, and Count Andrenyi has told us that his wife took a sleeping draught. Therefore it seems impossible that it can be anybody – which is absurd!'

'As our old friend Euclid says,' murmured Poirot.

'It must be one of those four,' said Dr Constantine. 'Unless it is someone from outside who has found a hiding place – and that, we agreed, was impossible.'

M. Bouc had passed on to the next question on the list.

'No. 5 – why do the hands of the broken watch point to 1.15? I can see two explanations of that. Either it was done by the murderer to establish an alibi and afterwards he was prevented from leaving the compartment when he meant to do so by hearing people moving about, or else – wait – I have an idea coming –'

The other two waited respectfully while M. Bouc struggled in mental agony.

'I have it,' he said at last. 'It was *not* the Wagon Lit murderer who tampered with the watch! It was the person we have called the Second Murderer – the left-handed person – in other words the woman in the scarlet kimono. She arrives later and moves back the hands of the watch in order to make an alibi for herself.'

'Bravo,' said Dr Constantine. 'It is well imagined, that.'

'In fact,' said Poirot, 'she stabbed him in the dark, not realizing that he was dead already, but somehow deduced that he had a watch in his pyjama pocket, took it out, put back the hands blindly and gave it the requisite dent.'

M. Bouc looked at him coldly.

'Have you anything better to suggest yourself?' he asked.

'At the moment – no,' admitted Poirot.

'All the same,' he went on, 'I do not think you have either of you appreciated the most interesting point about that watch.'

'Does question No. 6 deal with it?' asked the doctor. 'To that question – was the murder committed at that time – 1.15 – I answer, "*No.*"'

'I agree,' said M. Bouc. '"Was it earlier?" is the next question. I say yes. You, too, doctor?'

The doctor nodded.

'Yes, but the question "Was it later?" can also be answered in the affirmative. I agree with your theory, M. Bouc, and so, I think, does M. Poirot, although he does not wish to commit himself. The First Murderer came earlier than 1.15, the Second Murderer came *after* 1.15. And as regards the question of left-handedness, ought we not to take steps to ascertain which of the passengers is left-handed?'

'I have not completely neglected that point,' said Poirot. 'You may have noticed that I made each passenger write either a signature or an address. That is not conclusive, because some people do certain actions with the right hand and others with the left. Some write right-handed, but play golf left-handed. Still it is something. Every person questioned took the pen in their right hand – with the exception of Princess Dragomiroff, who refused to write.'

'Princess Dragomiroff, impossible,' said M. Bouc.

'I doubt if she would have had the strength to inflict that particular left-handed blow,' said Dr Constantine dubiously. 'That particular wound had been inflicted with considerable force.'

'More force than a woman could use?'

'No, I would not say that. But I think more force than an elderly woman could display, and Princess Dragomiroff's physique is particularly frail.'

'It might be a question of the influence of mind over body,' said Poirot. 'Princess Dragomiroff has great personality and immense will power. But let us pass from that for the moment.'

'To questions Nos. 9 and 10. Can we be sure that

Ratchett was stabbed by more than one person, and what other explanation of the wounds can there be? In my opinion, medically speaking, there can be *no other* explanation of those wounds. To suggest that one man struck first feebly and then with violence, first with the right hand and then with the left, and after an interval of perhaps half an hour inflicted fresh wounds on a dead body – well, it does not make sense.'

'No,' said Poirot. 'It does not make sense. And you think that two murderers do make sense?'

'As you yourself have said, what other explanation can there be?'

Poirot stared straight ahead of him.

'That is what I ask myself,' he said. 'That is what I never cease to ask myself.'

He leaned back in his seat.

'From now on, it is all here,' he tapped himself on the forehead. 'We have thrashed it all out. The facts are all in front of us – neatly arranged with order and method. The passengers have sat here, one by one, giving their evidence. We know all that can be known – *from outside* . . .'

He gave an affectionate smile at M. Bouc.

'It has been a little joke between us, has it not – this business of sitting back and *thinking* out the truth? Well, I am about to put my theory into practice –

here before your eyes. You two must do the same. Let us all three close our eyes and *think* . . .'

'One or more of those passengers killed Ratchett. *Which of them?*'

Chapter 3

Certain Suggestive Points

It was quite a quarter of an hour before anyone spoke.

M. Bouc and Dr Constantine had started by trying to obey Poirot's instructions. They had endeavoured to see through the maze of conflicting particulars to a clear and outstanding solution.

M. Bouc's thoughts had run something as follows:

'Assuredly I must think. But as far as that goes I have already thought . . . Poirot obviously thinks this English girl is mixed up in the matter. I cannot help feeling that that is most unlikely . . . The English are extremely cold. Probably it is because they have no figures . . . But that is not the point. It seems that the Italian could not have done it – a pity. I suppose the English valet is not lying when he said the other never left the compartment? But why should he? It is not easy to bribe the English, they are so unapproachable. The whole thing is most unfortunate. I wonder when we shall get out of this. There must be *some* rescue work in progress. They are so slow in these countries . . . it is hours before anyone thinks of doing anything. And the police of these countries, they will be most trying to deal with – puffed up with importance, touchy, on their dignity. They will make a grand affair of all this. It is not often that such a chance comes their way. It will be in all the newspapers . . .'

And from there on M. Bouc's thoughts went along a well-worn course which they had already traversed some hundred times.

Dr Constantine's thoughts ran thus:

'He is queer, this little man. A genius? Or a crank? Will he solve this mystery? Impossible. I can see no way out of it. It is all too confusing . . . Everyone is lying, perhaps . . . But even then that does not help one. If they are all lying it is just as confusing as if they were speaking the truth. Odd about those wounds. I cannot understand it . . . It would be easier to understand if he had been shot – after all, the term gunman must mean that they shoot with a gun. A curious country, America. I should like to go there. It is so progressive. When I get home I must get hold of Demetrius Zagone – he has been to America, he has all the modern ideas . . . I wonder what Zia is doing at this moment. If my wife ever finds out –'

His thoughts went on to entirely private matters.

Hercule Poirot sat very still.

One might have thought he was asleep.

And then, suddenly, after a quarter of an hour's complete immobility, his eyebrows began to move slowly up his forehead. A little sigh escaped him. He murmured beneath his breath:

'But, after all, why not? And if so – why, if so, that would explain everything.'

His eyes opened. They were green like a cat's. He said softly:

'*Eh bien*. I have thought. And you?'

Lost in their reflections, both men started violently.

'I have thought also,' said M. Bouc just a shade guilty. 'But I have arrived at no conclusion. The elucidation of crime is your *métier*, not mine, my friend.'

'I, too, have reflected with great earnestness,' said the doctor unblushingly, recalling his thoughts from certain pornographic details. 'I have thought of many possible theories, but not one that really satisfies me.'

Poirot nodded amiably. His nod seemed to say:

'Quite right. That is the proper thing to say. You have given me the cue I expected.'

He sat very upright, threw out his chest, caressed his moustache and spoke in the manner of a practised speaker addressing a public meeting.

'My friends, I have reviewed the facts in my mind, and have also gone over to myself the evidence of the passengers – with this result. I see, nebulously as yet, a certain explanation that would cover the facts as we know them. It is a very curious explanation, and I cannot be sure as yet that it is the true one. To find out definitely, I shall have to make certain experiments.

'I would like first to mention certain points which appear to me suggestive. Let us start with a remark made to me by M. Bouc in this very place on the occasion of our first lunch together on the train. He commented on the fact that we were surrounded by people of all classes, of all ages, of all nationalities. That is a fact somewhat rare at this time of year. The Athens-Paris and the Bucharest-Paris coaches, for instance, are almost empty. Remember also one passenger who failed to turn up. It is, I think, significant. Then there are some minor points that strike me as suggestive – for instance, the position of Mrs Hubbard's sponge-bag, the name of Mrs Armstrong's mother, the detective methods of M. Hardman, the suggestion of M. MacQueen that Ratchett himself destroyed the charred note we found, Princess Dragomiroff's Christian name, and a grease spot on a Hungarian passport.'

The two men stared at him.

'Do they suggest anything to you, those points?' asked Poirot.

'Not a thing,' said M. Bouc frankly.

'And M. le docteur?'

'I do not understand in the least of what you are talking.'

M. Bouc, meanwhile, seizing upon the one tangible thing his friend had mentioned, was sorting through the passports. With a grunt he picked up that of Count and Countess Andrenyi and opened it.

'Is this what you mean? This dirty mark?'

'Yes. It is a fairly fresh grease spot. You notice where it occurs?'

'At the beginning of the description of the Count's wife – her Christian name, to be exact. But I confess that I still do not see the point.'

'I am going to approach it from another angle. Let us go back to the handkerchief found at the scene of the crime. As we have stated not long ago – three people are associated with the letter H. Mrs Hubbard, Miss Debenham and the maid, Hildegarde Schmidt. Now let us regard that handkerchief from another point of view. It is, my friends, an extremely expensive handkerchief – an *objet de luxe*, hand made, embroidered in Paris. Which of the passengers, apart from the initial, was likely to own such a handkerchief? Not Mrs Hubbard, a worthy woman with no pretensions to reckless extravagance in dress. Not Miss Debenham; that class of Englishwoman has a dainty linen handkerchief, but not an expensive wisp of cambric costing perhaps two hundred francs. And certainly not the maid. But there *are* two women on the train who would be likely to own such a handkerchief. Let us see if we can connect them in any way with the letter H. The two women I refer to are Princess Dragomiroff –'

'Whose Christian name is Natalia,' put in M. Bouc ironically.

'Exactly. And her Christian name, as I said just now, is decidedly suggestive. The other woman is Countess Andrenyi. And at once something strikes us –'

'*You!*'

'*Me*, then. Her Christian name on her passport is disfigured by a blob of grease. Just an accident, anyone would say. But consider that Christian name. Elena. Suppose that, instead of Elena, it were *Helena*. That capital H could be turned into a capital E and then run over the small e next to it quite easily – and then a spot of grease dropped to cover up the alteration.'

'Helena,' cried M. Bouc. 'It is an idea, that.'

'Certainly it is an idea! I look about for any confirmation, however slight, of my idea – and I find it. One of the luggage labels on the Countess's baggage is slightly damp. It is one that happens to run over the first initial on top of the case. That label has been soaked off and put on again in a different place.'

'You begin to convince me,' said M. Bouc, 'But the Countess Andrenyi – surely –'

'Ah, now, *mon vieux*, you must turn yourself round and approach an entirely different angle of the case. How was this murder intended to appear to everybody? Do not forget that the snow has upset all the murderer's original plan. Let us imagine, for a little minute, that there is no snow, that the train proceeded on its normal course. What, then, would have happened?

'The murder, let us say, would still have been discovered in all probability at the Italian frontier early this morning. Much of the same evidence would have been given to the Italian police. The threatening letters would have been produced by M. MacQueen, M. Hardman would have told his story, Mrs Hubbard would have been eager to tell how a man passed through her compartment, the button would have been found. I imagine that two things only would have been different. The man would have passed through Mrs Hubbard's compartment just before one o'clock – and the Wagon Lit uniform would have been found cast off in one of the toilets.'

'You mean?'

'I mean that the murder was *planned to look like an outside job*. The assassin would have been presumed to have left the train at Brod, where the train is timed to arrive at 00.58. Somebody would probably have passed a strange Wagon Lit conductor in the corridor. The

281

uniform would be left in a conspicuous place so as to show clearly just how the trick had been played. No suspicion would have been attached to the passengers. That, my friends, was how the affair was intended to appear to the outside world.

'But the accident to the train changes everything. Doubtless we have here the reason why the man remained in the compartment with his victim so long. He was waiting for the train to go on. But at last he realized *that the train was not going on*. Different plans would have to be made. The murderer would now be *known* to be still on the train.'

'Yes, yes,' said M. Bouc impatiently. 'I see all that. But where does the handkerchief come in?'

'I am returning to it by a somewhat circuitous route. To begin with, you must realize that the threatening letters were in the nature of a blind. They might have been lifted bodily out of an indifferently written American crime novel. They are not *real*. They are, in fact, simply intended for the police. What we have to ask ourselves is, "Did they deceive Ratchett?" On the face of it, the answer seems to be, "No." His instructions to Hardman seem to point to a definite "private" enemy of the identity of whom he was well aware. That is if we accept Hardman's story as true. But Ratchett certainly received *one* letter of a very different character – the one containing a reference to the Armstrong baby, a fragment of which we found in his compartment. In case Ratchett had not realized it sooner, this was to make sure that he understood the reason of the threats against his life. That letter, as I have said all along, was *not* intended to be found. The murderer's first care was to destroy it. This, then, was the second hitch in his plans. The first was the snow, the second was our reconstruction of that fragment.

'That note being destroyed so carefully can only mean one thing. *There must be on the train someone so intimately connected with the Armstrong family that the finding of that note would immediately direct suspicion upon that person.*

'Now we come to the other two clues that we found. I pass over the pipe-cleaner. We have already said a good deal about that. Let us pass on to the handkerchief. Taken at its simplest, it is a clue which directly incriminates someone whose initial is H, and it was dropped there unwittingly by that person.'

'Exactly,' said Dr Constantine. 'She finds out that she has dropped the handkerchief and immediately takes steps to conceal her Christian name.'

'How fast you go. You arrive at a conclusion much sooner than I would permit myself to do.'

'Is there any other alternative?'

'Certainly there is. Suppose, for instance, that you

have committed a crime and wish to cast suspicion for it on someone else. Well, there is on the train a certain person connected intimately with the Armstrong family – a woman. Suppose, then, that you leave there a handkerchief belonging to that woman. She will be questioned, her connection with the Armstrong family will be brought out – *et voilà*. Motive – *and* an incriminating article of evidence.'

'But in such a case,' objected the doctor, 'the person indicated being innocent, would not take steps to conceal her identity.'

'Ah, really? That is what you think? That is truly the opinion of the police court. But I know human nature, my friend, and I tell you that, suddenly confronted with the possibility of being tried for murder, the most innocent person will lose their head and do the most absurd things. No, no, the grease spot and the changed label do not prove guilt – they only prove that the Countess Andrenyi is anxious for some reason to conceal her identity.'

'What do you think her connection with the Armstrong family can be? She has never been in America, she says.'

'Exactly, and she speaks broken English, and she has a very foreign appearance which she exaggerates. But it should not be difficult to guess who she is. I mentioned just now the name of Mrs Armstrong's

mother. It was Linda Arden, and she was a very celebrated actress – among other things a Shakespearean
actress. Think of *As You Like It* – the Forest of Arden
and Rosalind. It was there she got the inspiration for
her acting name. Linda Arden, the name by which
she was known all over the world, was not her real
name. It may have been Goldenberg – she quite likely
had central European blood in her veins – a strain of
Jewish, perhaps. Many nationalities drift to America.
I suggest to you, gentlemen, that that young sister of
Mrs Armstrong's, little more than a child at the time
of the tragedy, was Helena Goldenberg the younger
daughter of Linda Arden, and that she married Count
Andrenyi when he was an attaché in Washington.'

'But Princess Dragomiroff says that she married an
Englishman.'

'Whose name she cannot remember! I ask you, my
friends – is that really likely? Princess Dragomiroff
loved Linda Arden as great ladies do love great artists.
She was godmother to one of her daughters. Would
she forget so quickly the married name of the other
daughter? It is not likely. No, I think we can safely
say that Princess Dragomiroff was lying. She knew
Helena was on the train, she had seen her. She realized
at once, as soon as she heard who Ratchett really was,
that Helena would be suspected. And so, when we
question her as to the sister she promptly lies – is

vague, cannot remember, but "thinks Helena married
an Englishman" – a suggestion as far away from the
truth as possible.'

One of the restaurant attendants came through the
door at the end and approached them. He addressed
M. Bouc.

'The dinner, Monsieur, shall I serve it? It is ready
some little time.'

M. Bouc looked at Poirot. The latter nodded.

'By all means, let dinner be served.'

The attendant vanished through the doors at the
other end. His bell could be heard ringing and his
voice upraised:

'Premier Service. Le dîner est servi. Premier dîner –
First Service.'

Chapter 4

The Grease Spot on a Hungarian Passport

Poirot shared a table with M. Bouc and the doctor.

The company assembled in the restaurant-car was a very subdued one. They spoke little. Even the loquacious Mrs Hubbard was unnaturally quiet. She murmured as she sat:

'I don't feel as though I've got the heart to eat anything,' and then partook of everything offered her, encouraged by the Swedish lady, who seemed to regard her as a special charge.

Before the meal was served Poirot had caught the chief attendant by the sleeve and murmured something to him. Constantine had a pretty good guess what the instructions had been, as he noticed that the Count and Countess Andrenyi were always served last and that at the end of the meal there was a delay in making out their bill. It therefore came about that the Count and Countess were the last left in the restaurant-car.

When they rose at length and moved in the direction of the door, Poirot sprang up and followed them.

'Pardon, Madame, you have dropped your handkerchief.'

He was holding out to her the tiny monogrammed square.

She took it, glanced at it, then handed it back to him.

'You are mistaken, Monsieur, that is not my handkerchief.'

'Not your handkerchief? Are you sure?'

'Perfectly sure, Monsieur.'

'And yet, Madame, it has your initial – the initial H.'

The Count made a sudden movement. Poirot ignored him. His eyes were fixed on the Countess's face.

Looking steadily at him she replied:

'I do not understand, Monsieur. My initials are E.A.'

'I think not. Your name is Helena – not Elena. Helena Goldenberg, the younger daughter of Linda Arden – Helena Goldenberg, the sister of Mrs Armstrong.'

There was a dead silence for a minute or two. Both the Count and Countess had gone deadly white. Poirot said in a gentler tone:

'It is of no use denying. That is the truth, is it not?'

The Count burst out furiously:

'I demand, Monsieur, by what right you –'

She interrupted him, putting up a small hand towards his mouth.

'No, Rudolph. Let me speak. It is useless to deny what this gentleman says. We had better sit down and talk the matter out.'

Her voice had changed. It still had the southern richness of tone, but it had become suddenly more clear cut and incisive. It was, for the first time, a definitely American voice.

The Count was silenced. He obeyed the gesture of her hand they both sat down opposite Poirot.

'Your statement, Monsieur, is quite true,' said the Countess. 'I am Helena Goldenberg, the younger sister of Mrs Armstrong.'

'You did not acquaint me with that fact this morning, Madame la Comtesse.'

'No.'

'In fact, all that your husband and you told me was a tissue of lies.'

'Monsieur,' cried the Count angrily.

'Do not be angry, Rudolph. M. Poirot puts the fact rather brutally, but what he says is undeniable.'

'I am glad you admit the fact so freely, Madame. Will you now tell me your reasons for so doing and also for altering your Christian name on your pass-port.'

'That was my doing entirely,' put in the Count.

Helena said quietly:

'Surely, M. Poirot, you can guess my reason – our reason. This man who was killed is the man who murdered my baby niece, who killed my sister, who broke my brother-in-law's heart. Three of the people I loved best and who made up my home – my world!'

Her voice rang out passionately. She was a true daughter of that mother, the emotional force of whose acting had moved huge audiences to tears.

She went on more quietly.

'Of all the people on the train, I alone had probably the best motive for killing him.'

'And you did not kill him, Madame?'

'I swear to you, M. Poirot, and my husband knows and will swear also – that, much as I may have been tempted to do so, I never lifted a hand against that man.'

'I too, gentlemen,' said the Count. 'I give you my word of honour that last night Helena never left her compartment. She took a sleeping draught exactly as I said. She is utterly and entirely innocent.'

Poirot looked from one to the other of them.

'On my word of honour,' repeated the Count.

Poirot shook his head slightly.

'And yet you took it upon yourself to alter the name in the passport?'

'Monsieur Poirot,' the Count spoke earnestly and passionately. 'Consider my position. Do you think I could stand the thought of my wife dragged through a sordid police case. She was innocent, I knew it, but what she said was true – because of her connection with the Armstrong family she would have been immediately suspected. She would have been questioned – arrested, perhaps. Since some evil chance had taken us on the same train as this man Ratchett, there was, I felt sure, but one thing for it. I admit, Monsieur, that I lied to you – all, that is, save in one thing. My wife never left her compartment last night.'

He spoke with an earnestness that it was hard to gainsay.

'I do not say that I disbelieve you, Monsieur,' said Poirot slowly. 'Your family is, I know, a proud and ancient one. It would be bitter indeed for you to have your wife dragged into an unpleasant police case. With that I can sympathize. But how, then, do you explain the presence of your wife's handkerchief actually in the dead man's compartment?'

'That handkerchief is not mine, Monsieur,' said the Countess.

'In spite of the initial H?'

'In spite of the initial. I have handkerchiefs not unlike

that, but not one that is exactly of that pattern. I know, of course that I cannot hope to make you believe me, but I assure you that it is so. That handkerchief is not mine.'

'It may have been placed there by someone in order to incriminate you?'

She smiled a little.

'You are enticing me to admit that, after all, it is mine? But indeed, M. Poirot, it isn't.'

She spoke with great earnestness.

'Then why, if the handkerchief was not yours, did you alter the name in the passport?'

The Count answered this.

'Because we heard that a handkerchief had been found with the initial H on it. We talked the matter over together before we came to be interviewed. I pointed out to Helena that if it were seen that her Christian name began with an H she would immediately be subjected to much more rigorous questioning. And the thing was so simple – to alter Helena to Elena was easily done.'

'You have, M. le Comte, the makings of a very fine criminal,' remarked Poirot dryly. 'A great natural ingenuity, and an apparently remorseless determination to mislead justice.'

'Oh, no, no,' the girl leaned forward. 'M. Poirot, he's explained to you how it was.' She broke from French into English. 'I was scared – absolutely dead scared, you understand. It had been so awful – that time – and to have it all raked up again. And to be suspected and perhaps thrown into prison. I was just scared stiff, M. Poirot. Can't you understand at all?'

Her voice was lovely – deep – rich – pleading, the voice of the daughter of Linda Arden the actress.

Poirot looked gravely at her.

'If I am to believe you, Madame – and I do not say that I will *not* believe you – then you must help me.'

'Help you?'

'Yes. The reason for the murder lies in the past – in that tragedy which broke up your home and saddened your young life. Take me back into the past, Mademoiselle, that I may find there the link that explains the whole thing.'

'What can there be to tell you? They are all dead.' She repeated mournfully. 'All dead – all dead – Robert, Sonia – darling, darling Daisy. She was so sweet – so happy – she had such lovely curls. We were all just crazy about her.'

'There was another victim, Madame. An indirect victim, you might say.'

'Poor Susanne? Yes, I had forgotten about her. The police questioned her. They were convinced she had something to do with it. Perhaps she had – but if so, only innocently. She had, I believe, chatted idly with someone, giving information as to the time of Daisy's outings. The poor thing got terribly wrought up – she thought she was being held responsible.' She shuddered. 'She threw herself out of the window. Oh it was horrible.'

She buried her face in her hands.

'What nationality was she, Madame?'

'She was French.'

'What was her last name?'

'It's absurd, but I can't remember – we all called her Susanne. A pretty laughing girl. She was devoted to Daisy.'

'She was the nursery-maid, was she not?'

'Yes.'

'Who was the nurse?'

'She was a trained hospital nurse. Stengelberg her name was. She, too, was devoted to Daisy – and to my sister.'

'Now, Madame, I want you to think carefully before you answer this question. Have you, since you were on this train, seen anyone that you recognized?'

She stared at him.

'I? No, no one at all.'

'What about Princess Dragomiroff?'

'Oh, her? I know her, of course. I thought you meant anyone – anyone from – from that time.'

'So I did, Madame. Now think carefully. Some years

have passed, remember. The person might have altered their appearance.'

Helena pondered deeply. Then she said:

'No – I am sure – there is no one.'

'You yourself – you were a young girl at the time – did you have no one to superintend your studies or to look after you?'

'Oh, yes, I had a dragon – a sort of governess to me and secretary to Sonia combined. She was English or rather Scotch – a big, red-haired woman.'

'What was her name?'

'Miss Freebody.'

'Young or old?'

'She seemed frightfully old to me. I suppose she couldn't have been more than forty. Susanne, of course, used to look after my clothes and maid me.'

'And there were no other inmates of the house?'

'Only servants.'

'And you are certain – quite certain, Madame – that you have recognized no one on the train?'

She replied earnestly:

'No one, Monsieur. No one at all.'

Chapter 5

The Christian Name of Princess Dragomiroff

When the Count and Countess had departed, Poirot looked across at the other two.

'You see,' he said, 'we make progress.'

'Excellent work,' said M. Bouc cordially. 'For my part, I should never have dreamed of suspecting Count and Countess Andrenyi. I will admit I thought them quite *hors de combat*. I suppose there is no doubt that she committed the crime? It is rather sad. Still, they will not guillotine her. There are extenuating circumstances. A few years' imprisonment – that will be all.'

'In fact you are quite certain of her guilt.'

'My dear friend, surely there is no doubt of it? I thought your reassuring manner was only to smooth things over till we are dug out of the snow and the police take charge.'

'You do not believe the Count's positive assertion –

on his word of honour – that his wife is innocent?'

'*Mon cher* – naturally – what else *could* he say? He adores his wife. He wants to save her! He tells his lie very well – quite in the grand Seigneur manner, but what else than a lie could it be?'

'Well, you know, I had the preposterous idea that it might be the truth.'

'No, no. The handkerchief, remember. The handkerchief clinches the matter.'

'Oh, I am not so sure about the handkerchief. You remember, I always told you that there were two possibilities as to the ownership of the handkerchief.'

'All the same –'

M. Bouc broke off. The door at the end had opened, and Princess Dragomiroff entered the dining-car. She came straight to them and all three men rose to their feet.

She spoke to Poirot, ignoring the others.

'I believe, Monsieur,' she said, 'that you have a handkerchief of mine.'

Poirot shot a glance of triumph at the other two.

'Is this it, Madame?'

He produced the little square of fine cambric.

'That is it. It has my initial in the corner.'

'But, Madame la Princesse, that is the letter H,' said M. Bouc. 'Your Christian name – pardon me – is Natalia.'

She gave him a cold stare.

'That is correct, Monsieur. My handkerchiefs are always initialled in the Russian characters. H is N in Russian.'

M. Bouc was somewhat taken aback. There was something about this indomitable old lady which made him feel flustered and uncomfortable.

'You did not tell us that this handkerchief was yours at the inquiry this morning.'

'You did not ask me,' said the Princess dryly.

'Pray be seated, Madame,' said Poirot.

She sighed.

'I may as well, I suppose.'

She sat down.

'You need not make a long business of this, Messieurs. Your next question will be – how did my handkerchief come to be lying by a murdered man's body? My reply to that is that I have no idea.'

'You have really no idea.'

'None whatever.'

'You will excuse me, Madame, but how much can we rely upon the truthfulness of your replies?'

Poirot said the words very softly. Princess Dragomiroff answered contemptuously.

'I suppose you mean because I did not tell you that Helena Andrenyi was Mrs Armstrong's sister?'

'In fact you deliberately lied to us in the matter.'

'Certainly. I would do the same again. Her mother was my friend. I believe, Messieurs, in loyalty – to one's friends and one's family and one's caste.'

'You do not believe in doing your utmost to further the ends of justice?'

'In this case I consider that justice – strict justice – has been done.'

Poirot leaned forward.

'You see my difficulty, Madame. In this matter of the handkerchief, even, am I to believe you? Or are you shielding your friend's daughter?'

'Oh! I see what you mean.' Her face broke into a grim smile. 'Well, Messieurs, this statement of mine can be easily proved. I will give you the address of the people in Paris who make my handkerchiefs. You have only to show them the one in question and they will inform you that it was made to my order over a year ago. The handkerchief is mine, Messieurs.'

She rose.

'Have you anything further you wish to ask me?'

'Your maid, Madame, did she recognize this handkerchief when we showed it to her this morning?'

'She must have done so. She saw it and said nothing? Ah, well, that shows that she too can be loyal.'

With a slight inclination of her head she passed out of the dining-car.

'So that was it,' murmured Poirot softly. 'I noticed

just a trifling hesitation when I asked the maid if she knew to whom the handkerchief belonged. She was uncertain whether or not to admit that it was her mistress's. But how does that fit in with that strange central idea of mine? Yes, it might well be.'

'Ah!' said M. Bouc with a characteristic gesture – 'she is a terrible old lady, that!'

'Could she have murdered Ratchett?' asked Poirot of the doctor.

He shook his head.

'Those blows – the ones delivered with great force penetrating the muscle – never, never could anyone with so frail a physique inflict them.'

'But the feebler ones?'

'The feebler ones, yes.'

'I am thinking,' said Poirot, 'of the incident this morning when I said to her that the strength was in her will rather than in her arm. It was in the nature of a trap, that remark. I wanted to see if she would look down at her right or her left arm. She did neither. She looked at them both. But she made a strange reply. She said, "No, I have no strength in these. I do not know whether to be sorry or glad." A curious remark that. It confirms me in my belief about the crime.'

'It did not settle the point about the left-handedness.'

'No. By the way, did you notice that Count Andrenyi

keeps his handkerchief in his right-hand breast pocket?'

M. Bouc shook his head. His mind reverted to the astonishing revelations of the last half-hour. He murmured:

'Lies – and again lies – it amazes me, the amount of lies we had told to us this morning.'

'There are more still to discover,' said Poirot cheerfully.

'You think so?'

'I shall be very disappointed if it is not so.'

'Such duplicity is terrible,' said M. Bouc. 'But it seems to please you,' he added reproachfully.

'It has this advantage,' said Poirot. 'If you confront anyone who has lied with the truth, they usually admit it – often out of sheer surprise. It is only necessary to guess *right* to produce your effect.

'That is the only way to conduct this case. I select each passenger in turn, consider their evidence and say to myself, "*If* so and so is lying, on what point are they lying and what is the *reason* for the lie?" And I answer *if* they are lying – *if*, you mark – it could only be for such a reason and on such a point. We have done that once very successfully with Countess Andrenyi. We shall now proceed to try the same method on several other persons.'

'And supposing, my friend, that your guess happens to be wrong?'

'Then one person, at any rate, will be completely freed from suspicion.'

'Ah! A process of elimination.'

'Exactly.'

'And who do we tackle next?'

'We are going to tackle that *pukka sahib*, Colonel Arbuthnot.'

Chapter 6

A Second Interview with
Colonel Arbuthnot

Colonel Arbuthnot was clearly annoyed at being summoned to the dining-car for a second interview. His face wore a most forbidding expression as he sat down and said:

'Well?'

'All my apologies for troubling you a second time,' said Poirot. 'But there is still some information that I think you might be able to give us.'

'Indeed? I hardly think so.'

'To begin with, you see this pipe-cleaner?'

'Yes.'

'Is it one of yours?'

'Don't know. I don't put a private mark on them, you know.'

'Are you aware, Colonel Arbuthnot, that you are the only man amongst the passengers in the Stamboul-

Calais carriage who smokes a pipe?'

'In that case it probably is one of mine.'

'Do you know where it was found?'

'Not the least idea.'

'It was found by the body of the murdered man.'

Colonel Arbuthnot raised his eyebrows.

'Can you tell us, Colonel Arbuthnot, how it is likely to have got there?'

'If you mean did I drop it there myself, no, I didn't.'

'Did you go into Mr Ratchett's compartment at any time?'

'I never even spoke to the man.'

'You never spoke to him and you did not murder him?'

The Colonel's eyebrows went up again sardonically.

'If I had, I should hardly be likely to acquaint you with the fact. As a matter of fact I *didn't* murder the fellow.'

'Ah, well,' murmured Poirot. 'It is of no consequence.'

'I beg your pardon?'

'I said that it was of no consequence.'

'Oh!' Arbuthnot looked taken aback. He eyed Poirot uneasily.

'Because, you see,' continued the little man, 'the pipe-cleaner, it is of no importance. I can myself think of eleven other excellent explanations of its presence.'

Arbuthnot stared at him.

'What I really wished to see you about was quite another matter,' went on Poirot. 'Miss Debenham may have told you, perhaps, that I overheard some words spoken to you at the station of Konya?'

Arbuthnot did not reply.

'She said, "*Not now. When it's all over. When it's behind us.*" Do you know to what those words referred?'

'I am sorry, M. Poirot, but I must refuse to answer that question.'

'*Pourquoi?*'

The Colonel said stiffly:

'I suggest that you should ask Miss Debenham herself for the meaning of those words.'

'I have done so.'

'And she refused to tell you?'

'Yes.'

'Then I should think it would have been perfectly plain – even to you – that my lips are sealed.'

'You will not give away a lady's secret?'

'You can put it that way, if you like.'

'Miss Debenham told me that they referred to a private matter of her own.'

'Then why not accept her word for it?'

'Because, Colonel Arbuthnot, Miss Debenham is what one might call a highly suspicious character.'

'Nonsense,' said the Colonel with warmth.

'It is not nonsense.'

'You have nothing whatever against her.'

'Not the fact that Miss Debenham was companion governess in the Armstrong household at the time of the kidnapping of little Daisy Armstrong?'

There was a minute's dead silence.

Poirot nodded his head gently.

'You see,' he said, 'we know more than you think. If Miss Debenham is innocent, why did she conceal that fact? Why did she tell me that she had never been in America?'

The Colonel cleared his throat.

'Aren't you possibly making a mistake?'

'I am making no mistake. Why did Miss Debenham lie to me?'

Colonel Arbuthnot shrugged his shoulders.

'You had better ask her. I still think that you are wrong.'

Poirot raised his voice and called. One of the restaurant attendants came from the far end of the car.

'Go and ask the English lady in No. 11 if she will be good enough to come here.'

'*Bien, Monsieur.*'

The man departed. The four men sat in silence. Colonel Arbuthnot's face looked as though it were carved out of wood, it was rigid and impassive.

The man returned.

'Thank you.'

A minute or two later Mary Debenham entered the dining-car.

Chapter 7

The Identity of Mary Debenham

She wore no hat. Her head was thrown back as though in defiance. The sweep of her hair back from her face, the curve of her nostril suggested the figurehead of a ship plunging gallantly into a rough sea. In that moment she was beautiful.

Her eyes went to Arbuthnot for a minute – just a minute.

She said to Poirot?

'You wished to see me?'

'I wished to ask you, Mademoiselle, why you lied to us this morning?'

'Lied to you? I don't know what you mean.'

'You concealed the fact that at the time of the Armstrong tragedy you were actually living in the house. You told me that you had never been in America.'

He saw her flinch for a moment and then recover herself.

'Yes,' she said. 'That is true.'

'No, Mademoiselle, it was false.'

'You misunderstood me. I mean that it is true that I lied to you.'

'Ah, you admit it?'

Her lips curved into a smile.

'Certainly. Since you have found me out.'

'You are at least frank, Mademoiselle.'

'There does not seem anything else for me to be.'

'Well, of course, that is true. And now, Mademoiselle, may I ask you the reason for these evasions?'

'I should have thought the reason leapt to the eye, M. Poirot?'

'It does not leap to mine, Mademoiselle.'

She said in a quiet, even voice with a trace of hardness in it:

'I have my living to get.'

'You mean –?'

She raised her eyes and looked him full in the face.

'How much do you know, M. Poirot, of the fight to get and keep decent employment? Do you think that a girl who had been detained in connection with a murder case, whose name and perhaps photographs were reproduced in the English papers – do you think that any nice ordinary middle-class Englishwoman would want to engage that girl as governess to her daughters?'

'I do not see why not – if no blame attached to you.'

'Oh, blame – it is not blame – it is publicity! So far, M. Poirot, I have succeeded in life. I have had well-paid, pleasant posts. I was not going to risk the position I had attained when no good end could have been served.'

'I will venture to suggest, Mademoiselle, that I would have been the best judge of that, not you.'

She shrugged her shoulders.

'For instance, you could have helped me in the matter of identification.'

'What do you mean?'

'Is it possible, Mademoiselle, that you did not recognize in the Countess Andrenyi Mrs Armstrong's young sister whom you taught in New York?'

'Countess Andrenyi? No.' She shook her head. 'It may seem extraordinary to you, but I did not recognize her. She was not grown up, you see, when I knew her. That was over three years ago. It is true that the Countess reminded me of someone – it puzzled me. But she looks so foreign – I never connected her with the little American schoolgirl. It is true that I only glanced at her casually when coming into the restaurant-car. I noticed her clothes more than her face –' she smiled faintly – 'women do! And then – well, I had my own preoccupations.'

'You will not tell me your secret, Mademoiselle?'

Poirot's voice was very gentle and persuasive.

She said in a low voice:

'I can't – I can't.'

And suddenly, without warning she broke down, dropping her face down upon her outstretched arms and crying as though her heart would break.

The Colonel sprang up and stood awkwardly beside her.

'I – look here –'

He stopped and, turning round, scowled fiercely at Poirot.

'I'll break every bone in your damned body, you dirty little whipper-snapper,' he said.

'Monsieur,' protested M. Bouc.

Arbuthnot had turned back to the girl.

'Mary – for God's sake –'

She sprang up.

'It's nothing. I'm all right. You don't need me any more, do you, M. Poirot? If you do, you must come and find me. Oh, what an idiot – what an idiot I'm making of myself!'

She hurried out of the car. Arbuthnot, before following her, turned once more on Poirot.

'Miss Debenham's got nothing to do with this business – nothing, do you hear? And if she's worried and interfered with, you'll have me to deal with.'

He strode out.

'I like to see an angry Englishman,' said Poirot. 'They are very amusing. The more emotional they feel the less command they have of language.'

But M. Bouc was not interested in the emotional reactions of Englishmen. He was overcome by admiration of his friend.

'*Mon cher, vous êtes épatant,*' he cried. 'Another miraculous guess. *C'est formidable.*'

'It is incredible how you think of these things,' said Dr Constantine admiringly.

'Oh, I claim no credit this time. It was not a guess. Countess Andrenyi practically told me.'

'*Comment*? Surely not?'

'You remember I asked her about her governess or companion? I had already decided in my mind that *if* Mary Debenham were mixed up in the matter, she must have figured in the household in some such capacity.'

'Yes, but the Countess Andrenyi described a totally different person.'

'Exactly. A tall, middle-aged woman with red hair – in fact, the exact opposite in every respect of Miss Debenham, so much so as to be quite remarkable. But then she had to invent a name quickly, and there it was that the unconscious association of ideas gave her away. She said Miss Freebody, you remember.'

'Yes?'

'*Eh bien*, you may not know it, but there is a shop in London that was called, until recently, Debenham & Freebody. With the name Debenham running in her head, the Countess clutches at another name quickly, and the first that comes is Freebody. Naturally I understood immediately.'

'That is yet another lie. Why did she do it?'

'Possibly more loyalty. It makes things a little difficult.'

'*Ma foi*,' said M. Bouc with violence. 'But does everybody on this train tell lies?'

'That,' said Poirot, 'is what we are about to find out.'

Chapter 8

Further Surprising Revelations

'Nothing would surprise me now,' said M. Bouc. 'Nothing! Even if everybody in the train proved to have been in the Armstrong household I should not express surprise.'

'That is a very profound remark,' said Poirot. 'Would you like to see what your favourite suspect, the Italian, has to say for himself?'

'You are going to make another of these famous guesses of yours?'

'Precisely.'

'It is really a *most* extraordinary case,' said Constantine.

'No, it is most natural.'

M. Bouc flung up his arms in comic despair.

'If this is what you call natural, *mon ami* –'

Words failed him.

Poirot had by this time requested the dining-car attendant to fetch Antonio Foscarelli.

The big Italian had a wary look in his eye as he came in. He shot nervous glances from side to side like a trapped animal.

'What do you want?' he said. 'I have nothing to tell you – nothing, do you hear! *Per Dio* –' He struck his hand on the table.

'Yes, you have something more to tell us,' said Poirot firmly. 'The truth!'

'The truth?' He shot an uneasy glance at Poirot. All the assurance and geniality had gone out of his manner.

'*Mais oui.* It may be that I know it already. But it will be a point in your favour if it comes from you spontaneously.'

'You talk like the American police. "Come clean," that is what they say – "come clean."'

'Ah! so you have had experience of the New York police?'

'No, no, never. They could not prove a thing against me – but it was not for want of trying.'

Poirot said quietly:

'That was in the Armstrong case, was it not? You were the chauffeur?'

His eyes met those of the Italian. The bluster went out of the big man. He was like a pricked balloon.

'Since you know – why ask me?'

'Why did you lie this morning?'

'Business reasons. Besides, I do not trust the Yugo-Slav police. They hate the Italians. They would not have given me justice.'

'Perhaps it is exactly justice that they *would* have given you!'

'No, no, I had nothing to do with this business last night. I never left my carriage. The long-faced Englishman, he can tell you so. It was not I who killed this pig – this Ratchett. You cannot prove anything against me.'

Poirot was writing something on a sheet of paper. He looked up and said quietly?

'Very good. You can go.'

Foscarelli lingered uneasily.

'You realize that it was not I – that I could have had nothing to do with it?'

'I said that you could go.'

'It is a conspiracy. You are going to frame me? All for a pig of a man who should have gone to the chair! It was an infamy that he did not. If it had been me – if I had been arrested –'

'But it was not you. You had nothing to do with the kidnapping of the child.'

'What is that you are saying? Why, that little one – she was the delight of the house. Tonio, she called me. And she would sit in the car and pretend to hold the wheel. All the household worshipped her! Even the police came to understand that. Ah, the beautiful little one.'

His voice had softened. The tears came into his eyes. Then he wheeled round abruptly on his heel and strode out of the dining-car.

'Pietro,' called Poirot.

The dining-car attendant came at a run.

'The No. 10 – the Swedish lady.'

'*Bien, Monsieur.*'

'Another?' cried M. Bouc. 'Ah, no – it is not possible. I tell you it is not possible.'

'*Mon cher*, we have to know. Even if in the end everybody on the train proves to have a motive for killing Ratchett, we have to know. Once we know, we can settle once for all where the guilt lies.'

'My head is spinning,' groaned M. Bouc.

Greta Ohlsson was ushered in sympathetically by the attendant. She was weeping bitterly.

She collapsed on the seat facing Poirot and wept steadily into a large handkerchief.

'Now do not distress yourself, Mademoiselle. Do not distress yourself.' Poirot patted her on the shoulder. 'Just a few little words of truth, that is all. You were the nurse who was in charge of little Daisy Armstrong?'

'It is true – it is true,' wept the wretched woman. 'Ah, she was an angel – a little sweet, trustful angel. She knew nothing but kindness and love – and she was taken away by that wicked man – cruelly treated – and her poor mother – and the other little one who never lived at all. You cannot understand – you cannot know – if you had been there as I was – if you had seen the whole terrible tragedy – I ought to have told you the truth about myself this morning. But I was afraid – afraid. I did so rejoice that that evil man was dead – that he could not any more kill or torture little children. Ah! I cannot speak – I have no words . . .'

She wept with more vehemence than ever.

Poirot continued to pat her gently on the shoulder.

'There – there – I comprehend – I comprehend everything – everything, I tell you. I will ask you no more questions. It is enough that you have admitted what I know to be the truth. I understand, I tell you.'

By now inarticulate with sobs, Greta Ohlsson rose and groped her way blindly towards the door. As she reached it she collided with a man coming in.

It was the valet – Masterman.

He came straight up to Poirot and spoke in his usual, quiet, unemotional voice.

'I hope I'm not intruding, sir. I thought it best to come along at once, sir, and tell you the truth. I was Colonel Armstrong's batman in the war, sir, and afterwards I was his valet in New York. I'm afraid I concealed that fact this morning. It was very wrong of me, sir, and I thought I'd better come and make a clean breast of it. But I hope, sir, that you're not suspecting Tonio in any way. Old Tonio, sir, wouldn't hurt a fly. And I can swear positively that he never left the carriage all last night. So, you see, sir, he couldn't have done it. Tonio may be a foreigner, sir, but he's a very gentle creature – not like those nasty murdering Italians one reads about.'

He stopped.

Poirot looked steadily at him.

'Is that all you have to say?'

'That is all, sir.'

He paused, then, as Poirot did not speak, he made an apologetic little bow, and after a momentary hesitation left the dining-car in the same quiet, unobtrusive fashion as he had come.

'This,' said Dr Constantine, 'is more wildly improbable than any *roman policier* I have ever read.'

'I agree,' said M. Bouc. 'Of the twelve passengers in that coach, nine have been proved to have had a connection with the Armstrong case. What next, I ask you? Or, should I say, who next?'

'I can almost give you the answer to your question,' said Poirot. 'Here comes our American sleuth, M. Hardman.'

'Is he, too, coming to confess?'

Before Poirot could reply, the American had reached

their table. He cocked an alert eye at them and, sitting down, he drawled out:

'Just exactly what's up on this train? It seems bughouse to me.'

Poirot twinkled at him:

'Are you quite sure, Mr Hardman, that you yourself were not the gardener at the Armstrong home?'

'They didn't have a garden,' replied Mr Hardman literally.

'Or the butler?'

'Haven't got the fancy manner for a place like that. No, I never had any connection with the Armstrong house – but I'm beginning to believe I'm about the only one on this train who hadn't! Can you beat it – that's what I say? Can you beat it?'

'It is certainly a little surprising,' said Poirot mildly.

'*C'est rigolo*,' burst from M. Bouc.

'Have you any ideas of your own about the crime, M. Hardman?' inquired Poirot.

'No, sir. It's got me beat. I don't know how to figure it out. They can't all be in it; but which one is the guilty party is beyond me. How did you get wise to all this, that's what I want to know?'

'I just guessed.'

'Then, believe me, you're a pretty slick guesser. Yes, I'll tell the world you're a slick guesser.'

Mr Hardman leaned back and looked at Poirot admiringly.

'You'll excuse me,' he said, 'but no one would believe it to look at you. I take off my hat to you. I do, indeed.'

'You are too kind, M. Hardman.'

'Not at all. I've got to hand it to you.'

'All the same,' said Poirot, 'the problem is not yet quite solved. Can we say with authority that we know who killed M. Ratchett?'

'Count me out,' said Mr Hardman. 'I'm not saying anything at all. I'm just full of natural admiration. What about the other two you've not had a guess at yet? The old American dame and the lady's-maid? I suppose we can take it that they're the only innocent parties on the train?'

'Unless,' said Poirot, smiling, 'we can fit them into our little collection as – shall we say? – housekeeper and cook in the Armstrong household.'

'Well, nothing in the world would surprise me now,' said Mr Hardman with quiet resignation. 'Bughouse – that's what this business is – bughouse!'

'Ah, *mon cher*, that would be indeed stretching coincidence a little too far,' said M. Bouc. 'They cannot all be in it.'

Poirot looked at him.

'You do not understand,' he said. 'You do not

understand at all. Tell me,' he said, 'do you know who killed Ratchett?'

'Do you?' countered M. Bouc.

Poirot nodded.

'Oh, yes,' he said. 'I have known for some time. It is so clear that I wonder you have not seen it also.' He looked at Hardman and asked, 'And you?'

The detective shook his head. He stared at Poirot curiously.

'I don't know,' he said. 'I don't know at all. Which of them was it?'

Poirot was silent a minute. Then he said:

'If you will be so good, M. Hardman, assemble everyone here. There are two possible solutions of this case. I want to lay them both before you all.'

Chapter 9

Poirot Propounds Two Solutions

The passengers came crowding into the restaurant-car and took their seats round the tables. They all bore more or less the same expression, one of expectancy mingled with apprehension. The Swedish lady was still weeping and Mrs Hubbard was comforting her.

'Now you must just take a hold on yourself, my dear. Everything's going to be perfectly all right. You mustn't lose your grip on yourself. If one of us is a nasty murderer we know quite well it isn't you. Why, anyone would be crazy even to think of such a thing. You sit here and I'll stay right by you; and don't you worry any.'

Her voice died away as Poirot stood up.

The Wagon Lit conductor was hovering in the doorway.

'You permit that I stay, Monsieur?'

'Certainly, Michel.'

Poirot cleared his throat.

'Messieurs et Mesdames, I will speak in English, since I think all of you know a little of that language. We are here to investigate the death of Samuel Edward Ratchett – alias Cassetti. There are two possible solutions of the crime. I shall put them both before you, and I shall ask M. Bouc and Dr Constantine here to judge which solution is the right one.

'Now you all know the facts of the case. Mr Ratchett was found stabbed this morning. He was last known to be alive at 12.37 last night, when he spoke to the Wagon Lit conductor through the door. A watch in his pyjama pocket was found to be badly dented and it had stopped at a quarter-past one. Dr Constantine, who examined the body when found, puts the time of death as having occurred between midnight and two in the morning. At half an hour after midnight, as you all know, the train ran into a snowdrift. After that time it *was impossible for anyone to leave the train*.

'The evidence of Mr Hardman, who is a member of a New York Detective Agency' (several heads turned to look at Mr Hardman) 'shows that no one could have passed his compartment (No. 16 at the extreme end) without being seen by him. We are therefore forced to the conclusion that the murderer is to be found among the occupants of one particular coach – the Stamboul-Calais coach.

'That, I will say, *was* our theory.'

'*Comment*?' ejaculated M. Bouc, startled.

'But I will put before you an alternative theory. It is very simple. Mr Ratchett had a certain enemy whom he feared. He gave Mr Hardman a description of this enemy and told him that the attempt, if made at all, would most probably be made on the second night out from Stamboul.

'Now I put it to you, ladies and gentlemen, that Mr Ratchett knew a good deal more than he told. The enemy as Mr Ratchett expected, joined the train at *Belgrade, or possibly at Vincovci*, by the door left open by Colonel Arbuthnot and Mr MacQueen who had just descended to the platform. He was provided with a suit of Wagon Lit uniform, which he wore over his ordinary clothes, and a pass key which enabled him to gain access to Mr Ratchett's compartment in spite of the door being locked. Mr Ratchett was under the influence of a sleeping draught. This man stabbed him with great ferocity and left the compartment through the communicating door leading to Mrs Hubbard's compartment –'

'That's so,' said Mrs Hubbard, nodding her head.

'He thrust the dagger he had used into Mrs Hubbard's sponge-bag in passing. Without knowing it, he lost a button of his uniform. Then he slipped out of the compartment and along the corridor. He hastily thrust the uniform into a suitcase in an empty compartment, and a few minutes later, dressed in ordinary clothes, he left the train just before it started off. Again using the same means of egress – the door near the dining-car.'

Everybody gasped.

'What about that watch?' demanded Mr Hardman.

'There you have the explanation of the whole thing. *Mr Ratchett had ommitted to put his watch back an hour as he should have done* at Tzaribrod. His watch still registered Eastern European time, which is one hour *ahead* of Central European time. It was a quarter-past *twelve* when Mr Ratchett was stabbed – not a quarter-past one.'

'But it is absurd, that explanation,' cried M. Bouc. 'What of the voice that spoke from the compartment at twenty-three minutes to one. It was either the voice of Ratchett – or else of his murderer.'

'Not necessarily. It might have been – well – a third person. One who had gone in to speak to Ratchett and found him dead. He rang the bell to summon the conductor, then, as you express it, the wind rose in him – he was afraid of being accused of the crime and he spoke pretending to be Ratchett.'

'*C'est possible*,' admitted M. Bouc grudgingly.

Poirot looked at Mrs Hubbard.

'Yes, Madame, you were going to say –?'

'Well, I don't quite know what I was going to

say. Do you think I forgot to put my watch back too?'

'No, Madame. I think you heard the man pass through – but unconsciously; later you had a nightmare of a man being in your compartment and woke up with a start and rang for the conductor.'

'Well, I suppose that's possible,' admitted Mrs Hubbard.

Princess Dragomiroff was looking at Poirot with a very direct glance.

'How do you explain the evidence of my maid, Monsieur?'

'Very simply, Madame. Your maid recognized the handkerchief I showed her as yours. She somewhat clumsily tried to shield you. She did encounter the man – but earlier – while the train was at Vincovci station. She pretended to have seen him at a later hour with a confused idea of giving you a watertight *alibi*.'

The Princess bowed her head.

'You have thought of everything, Monsieur. I – I admire you.'

There was a silence.

Then everyone jumped as Dr Constantine suddenly hit the table a blow with his fist.

'But no,' he said. 'No, no, and again no! That is an explanation that will not hold water. It is deficient in a dozen minor points. The crime was not committed so – M. Poirot must know that perfectly well.'

Poirot turned a curious glance on him.

'I see,' he said, 'that I shall have to give my second solution. But do not abandon this one too abruptly. You may agree with it later.'

He turned back again to face the others.

'There is another possible solution of the crime. This is how I arrived at it.

'When I had heard all the evidence, I leaned back and shut my eyes and began to *think*. Certain points presented themselves to me as worthy of attention. I enumerated these points to my two colleagues. Some I have already elucidated – such as a grease-spot on a passport, etc. I will run over the points that remain. The first and most important is a remark made to me by M. Bouc in the restaurant-car at lunch on the first day after leaving Stamboul – to the effect that the company assembled was interesting because it was so varied – representing as it did all classes and nationalities.

'I agreed with him, but when this particular point came into my mind, I tried to imagine whether such an assembly were ever likely to be collected under any other conditions. And the answer I made to myself was – only in America. In America there might be a household composed of just such varied nationalities –

an Italian chauffeur, and English governess, a Swedish nurse, a French lady's-maid and so on. That led me to my scheme of "guessing" – that is, casting each person for a certain part in the Armstrong drama much as a producer casts a play. Well, that gave me an extremely interesting and satisfactory result.

'I had also examined in my own mind each separate person's evidence with some curious results. Take first the evidence of Mr MacQueen. My first interview with him was entirely satisfactory. But in my second he made rather a curious remark. I had described to him the finding of a note mentioning the Armstrong case. He said, "But surely –" and then paused and went on, "I mean – that was rather careless of the old man."

'Now I could feel that that was not what he had started out to say. *Supposing what he had meant to say was, "But surely that was burnt!"* In which case, *MacQueen knew of the note and of its destruction* – in other words, he was either the murderer or an accomplice of the murderer. Very good.

'Then the valet. He said his master was in the habit of taking a sleeping draught when travelling by train. That might be true, but *would Ratchett have taken one last night?* The automatic under his pillow gave the lie to that statement. Ratchett intended to be on the alert last night. Whatever narcotic was administered to him must have been done so without his knowledge. By whom? Obviously by MacQueen or the valet.

'Now we come to the evidence of Mr Hardman. I believed all that he told me about his own identity, but when it came to the actual methods he had employed to guard Mr Ratchett, his story was neither more nor less than absurd. The only way effectively to have protected Ratchett was to have passed the night actually in his compartment or in some spot where he could watch the door. The only thing that his evidence *did* show plainly was that no one *in any other part of the train could possibly have murdered Ratchett*. It drew a clear circle round the Stamboul-Calais carriage. That seemed to me a rather curious and inexplicable fact, and I put it aside to think over.

'You probably have all heard by now of the few words I overheard between Miss Debenham and Colonel Arbuthnot. The interesting thing to my mind was the fact that Colonel Arbuthnot called her *Mary* and was clearly on terms of intimacy with her. But the Colonel was only supposed to have met her a few days previously – and I know Englishmen of the Colonel's type. Even if he had fallen in love with the young lady at first sight, he would have advanced slowly and with decorum – not rushing things. Therefore I concluded that Colonel Arbuthnot and Miss Debenham were in reality well acquainted, and were for some reason pretending to be strangers. Another small point was Miss Debenham's easy familiarity with the term "long distance" for a telephone call. Yet Miss Debenham had told me that she had never been in the States.

'To pass to another witness. Mrs Hubbard had told us that lying in bed she was unable to see whether the communicating door was bolted or not, and so asked Miss Ohlsson to see for her. Now, though her statement would have been perfectly true if she had been occupying compartments Nos. 2, 4, 12, or any *even* number – where the bolt is directly under the handle of the door – in the *uneven* numbers, such as compartment No. 3, the bolt is well *above* the handle and could not therefore be masked by the sponge-bag in the least. I was forced to the conclusion that Mrs Hubbard was inventing an incident that had never occurred.

'And here let me say just a word or two about *times*. To my mind, the really interesting point about the dented watch was the place where it was found – in Ratchett's pyjama pocket, a singularly uncomfortable and unlikely place to keep one's watch, especially as there is a watch "hook" provided just by the head of the bed. I felt sure, therefore, that the watch had been deliberately placed in the pocket and faked. The crime, then, was not committed at a quarter-past one.

'Was it, then, committed earlier? To be exact, at

twenty-three minutes to one? My friend M. Bouc
advanced as an argument in favour of it the loud
cry which awoke me from sleep. But if Ratchett were
heavily drugged *he could not have cried out*. If he had
been capable of crying out he would have been capable
of making some kind of a struggle to defend himself,
and there were no signs of any such struggle.

'I remembered that MacQueen had called attention,
not once but twice (and the second time in a very
blatant manner), to the fact that Ratchett could speak
no French. I came to the conclusion that the whole
business at twenty-three minutes to one was a comedy
played for my benefit! Anyone might see through
the watch business – it is a common enough device
in detective stories. They assumed that I *should* see
through it and that, pluming myself on my own clever-
ness, I would go on to assume that since Ratchett spoke
no French the voice I heard at twenty-three minutes to
one could not be his, and that Ratchett must be already
dead. But I am convinced that at twenty-three minutes
to one Ratchett was still lying in his drugged sleep.

'But the device has succeeded! I have opened my
door and looked out. I have actually heard the French
phrase used. If I am so unbelievably dense as not
to realize the significance of that phrase, it must be
brought to my attention. If necessary MacQueen can
come right out in the open. He can say, "Excuse me,

M. Poirot, *that can't have been Mr Ratchett speaking.*
He can't speak French."

'Now when was the real time of the crime? And who
killed him?

'In my opinion, and this is only an opinion, Ratchett
was killed at some time very close upon two o'clock,
the latest hour the doctor gives us as possible.

'As to who killed him –'

He paused, looking at his audience. He could not
complain of any lack of attention. Every eye was fixed
upon him. In the stillness you could have heard a
pin drop.

He went on slowly:

'I was particularly struck by the extraordinary difficulty of proving a case against any one person on
the train and on the rather curious coincidence that
in each case the testimony giving an alibi came from
what I might describe as an "unlikely" person. Thus
Mr MacQueen and Colonel Arbuthnot provided alibis
for each other – two persons between whom it seemed
most unlikely there should be any prior acquaintance-
ship. The same thing happened with the English valet
and the Italian, with the Swedish lady and the English
girl. I said to myself, "This is extraordinary – they
cannot *all* be in it!"

'And then, Messieurs, I saw light. They were *all* in
it. For so many people connected with the Armstrong

case to be travelling by the same train by a coincidence was not only unlikely, it was *impossible*. It must be not chance, but *design*. I remembered a remark of Colonel Arbuthnot's about trial by jury. A jury is composed of twelve people – there were twelve passengers – Ratchett was stabbed twelve times. And the thing that had worried me all along – the extraordinary crowd travelling in the Stamboul-Calais coach at a slack time of year was explained.

'Ratchett had escaped justice in America. There was no question as to his guilt. I visualized a self-appointed jury of twelve people who condemned him to death and were forced by exigencies of the case to be their own executioners. And immediately, on that assumption, the whole case fell into beautiful shining order.

'I saw it as a perfect mosaic, each person playing his or her allotted part. It was so arranged that if suspicion should fall on any one person, the evidence of one or more of the others would clear the accused person and confuse the issue. Hardman's evidence was necessary in case some outsider should be suspected of the crime and be unable to prove an alibi. The passengers in the Stamboul carriage were in no danger. Every minute detail of their evidence was worked out beforehand. The whole thing was a very cleverly-planned jig-saw puzzle, so arranged that every fresh piece of knowledge that came to light made the solution of the whole more difficult. As my friend M. Bouc remarked, the case seemed fantastically impossible! That was exactly the impression intended to be conveyed.

'Did this solution explain everything? Yes, it did. The nature of the wounds – each inflicted by a different person. The artificial threatening letters – artificial since they were unreal, written only to be produced as evidence. (Doubtless there were real letters, warning Ratchett of his fate, which MacQueen destroyed, substituting for them these others.) Then Hardman's story of being called in by Ratchett – a lie, of course, from beginning to end – the description of the mythical "small dark man with a womanish voice," a convenient description, since it had the merit of not incriminating any of the actual Wagon Lit conductors and would apply equally well to a man or a woman.

'The idea of stabbing is at first sight a curious one, but on reflection nothing would fit the circumstances so well. A dagger was a weapon that could be used by everyone – strong or weak – and it made no noise. I fancy, though I may be wrong, that each person in turn entered Ratchett's darkened compartment through that of Mrs Hubbard – and struck! They themselves would never know which blow actually killed him.

'The final letter which Ratchett had probably found on his pillow was carefully burnt. With no clue pointing to the Armstrong case, there would be absolutely no reason for suspecting any of the passengers on the train. It would be put down as an outside job, and the "small dark man with the womanish voice" would actually have been seen by one or more of the passengers leaving the train at Brod.

'I do not know exactly what happened when the conspirators discovered that that part of their plan was impossible owing to the accident to the train. There was, I imagine, a hasty consultation, and then they decided to go through with it. It was true that now one and all of the passengers were bound to come under suspicion, but that possibility had already been foreseen and provided for. The only additional thing to be done was to confuse the issue even further. Two so-called "clues" were dropped in the dead man's compartment – one incriminating Colonel Arbuthnot (who had the strongest alibi and whose connection with the Armstrong family was probably the hardest to prove) and the second clue, the handkerchief, incriminating Princess Dragomiroff, who by virtue of her social position, her particularly frail physique and the alibi given her by her maid and the conductor, was practically in an unassailable position. Further to confuse the issue, a "red herring" was drawn across the trail – the mythical woman in the red kimono. Again I am to bear witness to this woman's existence. There is a heavy bang at my door. I get up and look out – and see the scarlet kimono disappearing in the distance. A judicious selection of people – the conductor, Miss Debenham and MacQueen – will also have seen her. It was, I think, someone with a sense of humour who thoughtfully placed the scarlet kimono on the top of my suitcase whilst I was interviewing people in the dining-car. Where the garment came from in the first place I do not know. I suspect it is the property of Countess Andrenyi, since her luggage contained only a chiffon negligée so elaborate as to be more a tea gown than a dressing-gown.

'When MacQueen first learned that the letter which had been so carefully burnt had in part escaped destruction, and that the word Armstrong was exactly the word remaining, he must at once have communicated his news to the others. It was at this minute that the position of Countess Andrenyi became acute and her husband immediately took steps to alter the passport. It was their second piece of bad luck!

'They one and all agreed to deny utterly any connection with the Armstrong family. They knew I had no immediate means of finding out the truth, and they did not believe that I should go into the matter unless my suspicions were aroused against one particular person.

'Now there was one further point to consider. Allowing that my theory of the crime was the correct one, and

I believe that it *must* be the correct one, then obviously the Wagon Lit conductor himself must be privy to the plot. But if so, that gave us thirteen persons, not twelve. Instead of the usual formula, "Of so many people one is guilty," I was faced with the problem that of thirteen persons one and one only was innocent. Which was that person?

'I came to a very odd conclusion. I came to the conclusion that the person who had taken no part in the crime was the person who would be considered the most likely to do so. I refer to Countess Andrenyi. I was impressed by the earnestness of her husband when he swore to me solemnly on his honour that his wife never left her compartment that night. I decided that Count Andrenyi took, so to speak, his wife's place.

'If so, then Pierre Michel was definitely one of the twelve. But how could one explain his complicity? He was a decent man who had been many years in the employ of the Company – not the kind of man who could be bribed to assist in a crime. Then Pierre Michel must be involved in the Armstrong case. But that seemed very improbable. Then I remembered that the dead nursery-maid was French. Supposing that that unfortunate girl had been Pierre Michel's daughter. That would explain everything – it would also explain the place chosen for the staging of the crime. Were there any others whose part in the drama was not

clear? Colonel Arbuthnot I put down as a friend of
the Armstrongs. They had probably been through
the war together. The maid, Hildegarde Schmidt, I
could guess her place in the Armstrong household.
I am, perhaps, overgreedy, but I sense a good cook
instinctively. I laid a trap for her – she fell into it.
I said I knew she was a good cook. She answered,
"Yes, indeed, all my ladies have said so." But if you
are employed as a *lady's-maid* your employers seldom
have a chance of learning whether or not you are a
good cook.

'Then there was Hardman. He seemed quite definitely not to belong to the Armstrong household. I
could only imagine that he had been in love with the
French girl. I spoke to him of the charm of foreign
women – and again I obtained the reaction I was
looking for. Sudden tears came into his eyes, which
he pretended were dazzled by the snow.

'There remains Mrs Hubbard. Now Mrs Hubbard,
let me say, played the most important part in the
drama. By occupying the compartment communicating with that of Ratchett she was more open to suspicion than anyone else. In the nature of things she could
not have an alibi to fall back upon. To play the part
she played – the perfectly natural, slightly ridiculous
American fond mother – an artist was needed. But
there *was* an artist connected with the Armstrong

343

family – Mrs Armstrong's mother – Linda Arden, the actress . . .'

He stopped.

Then, in a soft rich dreamy voice, quite unlike the one she had used all the journey, Mrs Hubbard said:

'I always fancied myself in comedy parts.'

She went on still dreamily:

'That slip about the sponge-bag was silly. It shows you should always rehearse properly. We tried it on the way out – I was in an even number compartment then, I suppose. I never thought of the bolts being in different places.'

She shifted her position a little and looked straight at Poirot.

'You know all about it, M. Poirot. You're a very wonderful man. But even you can't quite imagine what it was like – that awful day in New York. I was just crazy with grief – so were the servants – and Colonel Arbuthnot was there, too. He was John Armstrong's best friend.'

'He saved my life in the war,' said Arbuthnot.

'We decided then and there – perhaps we were mad – I don't know – that the sentence of death that Cassetti had escaped had got to be carried out. There were twelve of us – or rather eleven – Susanne's father was over in France, of course. First we thought we'd draw lots as to who should do it, but in the end we decided on this way. It was the chauffeur, Antonio, who suggested it. Mary worked out all the details later with Hector MacQueen. He'd always adored Sonia – my daughter – and it was he who explained to us exactly how Cassetti's money had managed to get him off.

'It took a long time to perfect our plan. We had first to track Ratchett down. Hardman managed that in the end. Then we had to try to get Masterman and Hector into his employment – or at any rate one of them. Well, we managed that. Then we had a consultation with Susanne's father. Colonel Arbuthnot was very keen on having twelve of us. He seemed to think it made it more in order. He didn't like the stabbing idea much, but he agreed that it did solve most of our difficulties. Well, Susanne's father was willing. Susanne was his only child. We knew from Hector that Ratchett would be coming back from the East sooner or later by the Orient Express. With Pierre Michel actually working on that train, the chance was too good to be missed. Besides, it would be a good way of not incriminating any outsiders.

'My daughter's husband had to know, of course, and he insisted on coming on the train with her. Hector wangled it so that Ratchett selected the right day for travelling when Michel would be on duty. We meant to engage every carriage in the Stamboul-Calais coach, but unfortunately there was one carriage we couldn't get. It was reserved long beforehand for a director of the company. Mr Harris, of course, was a myth. But it would have been awkward to have any stranger in Hector's compartment. And then, at the last minute, *you* came . . .'

She stopped.

'Well,' she said. 'You know everything now, M. Poirot. What are you going to do about it? If it must all come out, can't you lay the blame upon me and me only? I would have stabbed that man twelve times willingly. It wasn't only that he was responsible for my daughter's death and her child's, and that of the other child who might have been alive and happy now. It was more than that. There had been other children before Daisy – there might be others in the future. Society had condemned him; we were only carrying out the sentence. But it's unnecessary to bring all these others into it. All these good faithful souls – and poor Michel – and Mary and Colonel Arbuthnot – they love each other . . .'

Her voice was wonderful echoing through the crowded space – that deep, emotional, heart-stirring voice that had thrilled many a New York audience.

Poirot looked at his friend.

'You are a director of the company, M. Bouc,' he said, 'What do you say?'

M. Bouc cleared his throat.

'In my opinion, M. Poirot,' he said, 'the first theory you put forward was the correct one – decidedly so. I suggest that that is the solution we offer to the Yugo-Slavian police when they arrive. You agree, Doctor?'

'Certainly I agree,' said Dr Constantine. 'As regards the medical evidence, I think – er – that I made one or two fantastic suggestions.'

'Then,' said Poirot, 'having placed my solution before you, I have the honour to retire from the case . . .'

Five Little Pigs

POIROT

Agatha Christie

Beautiful Caroline Crale was convicted of poisoning her husband, but just like the nursery rhyme, there were five other 'little pigs' who could have done it: Philip Blake (the stockbroker) who went to market; Meredith Blake (the amateur herbalist) who stayed at home; Elsa Greer (the three-time divorcee) who had her roast beef; Cecilia Williams (the devoted governess) who had none; and Angela Warren (the disfigured sister) who cried all the way home.

Sixteen years later, Caroline's daughter is determined to prove her mother's innocence, and Poirot just can't get that nursery rhyme out of his mind...

'Mrs Christie as usual puts a ring through the reader's nose and leads him to one of her smashing last-minute showdowns.'   *Observer*

'The answer to the riddle is brilliant.'
                                          Times Literary Supplement

Evil Under the Sun

POIROT

Agatha Christie

The beautiful bronzed body of Arlena Stuart lay face down on the beach. But strangely, there was no sun and Arlena was not sun-bathing... she had been strangled.

Ever since Arlena's arrival the air had been thick with sexual tension. Each of the guests had a motive to kill her, including Arlena's new husband, but Hercule Poirot suspects that this apparent 'crime of passion' conceals something more evil and pre-meditated altogether.

'She springs her secret like a land mine.'

Times Literary Supplement

Endless Night

Agatha Christie

Some are born to sweet delight,
Some are born to endless night

When penniless Michael Rogers discovered the beautiful house at Gypsy's Acre and then meets the heiress Ellie, it seems that all his dreams have come true at once. But he ignores an old woman warning of an ancient curse, and evil begins to stir in paradise.

As Michael soon learns: Gypsy's Acre is the place where fatal 'accidents' happen…

'One of the best things Agatha Christie has ever done.'
Sunday Times

And Then There Were None

Agatha Christie

THE WORLD'S BEST-SELLING MYSTERY,
OVER 100 MILLION COPIES SOLD

'*Ten…*'
Ten strangers are lured to an isolated island mansion off the Devon coast by a mysterious 'U.N.Owen'.
'*Nine…*'
At dinner a recorded message accuses each of them in turn of having a guilty secret, and by the end of the night one of the guests is dead.
'*Eight…*'
Stranded by a violent storm, and haunted by an ancient nursery rhyme counting down one by one… as one by one… they begin to die.
'*Seven…*'
Which amongst them is the killer and will any of them survive?

'One of the very best, most genuinely bewildering Christies.'
Observer

'Agatha Christie's masterpiece.'   *Spectator*

Lord Edgware Dies

POIROT

Agatha Christie

When Lord Edgware is found murdered the police are baffled. His estranged actress wife was seen to visit him just before his death and Poirot himself heard her brag of her plan to 'get rid' of him.

After all, how could Jane have stabbed Lord Edgware to death in his library at exactly the same time she was seen dining with friends? It's a case that almost proves to be too much for the great Hercule Poirot.

'The whole case is a triumph of Poirot's special qualities.'
Times Literary Supplement